monster talk

monster talk

a novel

Michael Jarmer

iUniverse, Inc.
Bloomington

Monster Talk
A Novel

iUniverse books may be ordered through booksellers or by contacting:

iUniverse
1663 Liberty Drive
Bloomington, IN 47403
www.iuniverse.com
1-800-Authors (1-800-288-4677)

Cover illustration by Curtis Settino.

ISBN: 978-1-4759-1595-2 (sc)
ISBN: 978-1-4759-1596-9 (hc)
ISBN: 978-1-4759-1597-6 (e)

Printed in the United States of America

iUniverse rev. date: 05/10/2012

To my mothers, with love and appreciation:
Shirley and Winnie

"Even if they were to leave Europe, and inhabit the deserts of the new world, yet one of the first results of those sympathies for which the daemon thirsted would be children, and a race of devils would be propagated upon the earth who might make the very existence of the species of man a condition precarious and full of terror."

"Even where the affections are not strongly moved by any superior excellence, the companions of our childhood always possess a certain power over our minds, which hardly any later friend can obtain."

—Mary Shelley's *Frankenstein*

Part One

Prologue: Of the Children of Monsters

They were not devils. They were children not unlike other children, except that they were the children of monsters. But they were none of them devils.

It happened that, on his way to ignite his own funeral pyre, having failed in his hopes to reconcile with his creator, having wasted the rest of his life afterward on revenge and hatred, hoping to be rid of this world and its misery once and for all, and cruising the tundra of the northern-most regions of the world on his tiny ice raft, suddenly, inspired perhaps by the beauty of this place despite its inhospitable climate, he had a change of heart: *I will make my own companion. I will have one more chance in life. I will give the universe one last opportunity to prove itself not completely vile and pitiless. I will make my own goddamn monster.* And, to cover a lot of ground quickly so that we can arrive where we are to begin this narrative, let us say that he set out to do this deed and was successful, and, not unlike the way his own creator imagined it would happen, he traveled with his wife to America, settled down obscurely in the desert of what is now called Arizona, and proceeded to propagate the "race of devils."

Time passed, as it will do. Two hundred and sixty-four years after the first awakening, the family line stopped momentarily, perhaps forever (only time would tell), in the body of a child.

Of a Race of Devils

On the first day of the new school year the children were asked to tell the class their names and to share something interesting about themselves, something that made them unique. A healthy, small-framed boy of about seven years, confident and clean with eyes full of a still, deep water, stood up in front of Mrs. Terhart's second grade class and said, as a matter of fact but with a reverence almost palpable, "Hello, my name is Victor, and I am named after the great Dr. Frankenstein. My great-granddaddy was his monster."

Most of his classmates believed him immediately and unconditionally, but some of them sniggered, and some others thus far in their young lives had no awareness of such a personage and only just vaguely recognized the name from some deep place in the recesses of their little memories. Everybody, though, knew what a monster was, and there were lots of questions.

"What did your great-granddaddy look like? Was he ugly?"

"If your great-grandaddy was a monster, why aren't you a monster?"

"How does a monster talk?"

"Talk like a monster!"

"Did your great-granddaddy eat people?"

"Do you eat people?"

"Are you crazy?"

Mrs. Terhart was not pleased.

Later, she kept Victor inside as the class spilled out onto the playground. He stood next to her shyly, and she, sitting in her teacher chair behind her teacher desk, held him close, hugged him about the shoulders, looked down at him sweetly. "Dear Victor. You are such a good boy. You do your work in class, you never get into trouble, you don't fight or swear or tease girls. You had such a successful time in first grade. Why did you tell the other children about Dr. Frankenstein?"

"I did what you asked, Mrs. Terhart. You asked us to share something interesting about ourselves."

"Yes, dear Victor, but I wanted you to tell the truth."

"It is the truth, Mrs. Terhart. Scout's honor." And Victor immediately began to cry.

She hugged him a little harder. "Sweetie, Victor, do not be sad. We'll work on this together, okay? Don't you worry about it for now. Okay?"

Victor loved her. "All right," he said, and he was off to join the other children on the playground.

As would any child who is not believed by the adults in his life when he is telling the truth, Victor felt a constant pang of frustration in his younger years. At home, he was taught to speak honestly about his feelings and about what he knew to be true. But when Mrs. Terhart called home one evening, he heard his mother say that she didn't know why Victor would be saying such things to other students, and that she would have a talk with him. And she did have a talk.

"But Mama," Victor said, "you have always taught me to be truthful."

"Yes, Victor, but no one will believe you. It makes sense, then, that you spare yourself the trouble of not being believed. In this case only, you need not share that story with others. It is not a lie to simply choose some other interesting thing to share."

"But Mama, it is the only interesting thing about me."

"No, Victor. There are a million interesting things about you."

"Name one."

And Victor's mother, Justine, paused for a good long time before speaking.

She could have said that her young son was wise beyond his years, that if it weren't for his stature and childlike features, if you closed your eyes, you might believe you were in the presence of another adult, quiet and thoughtful. She could have said that he, unlike any child Justine had ever known, had a tremendous capacity for love. She could have said that she thought he would be great someday. She could have said that he, more than any member of her family or any relative in memory, was certainly no devil, was no monster.

"You are smart and sweet and good. A good boy," she said finally.

And while Victor knew that there was nothing particularly interesting about that at all, his heart warmed, and for a second he was flooded with the euphoria a boy feels when he knows he is loved by his mother. And he resolved in that moment to keep his family's history to himself. But it had already been spoken once, and some things are not easily forgotten. It would follow him, doggedly, throughout his childhood and into his teenage years.

It began only days after that first show-and-tell, when some especially resourceful young cretins, who had pumped their parents for information and had even been introduced to Boris Karloff, walked around the playground in front of Victor like arthritic zombies, wooden and stiff, flinging their limbs, waving off fire, growling, and then laughing hysterically.

Victor had never seen an actual photograph or drawing of his great-grandparents. Of course, by the time he was a teenager, he would have read the Shelley tale repeatedly, handed down to him through generations as a kind of family Bible. It was the history of his race—or, as it could be argued, the story of his species. While the "novel" would work on him profoundly, he would find the images of his great-grandfather in this record unhelpful, because before he could handle nineteenth-century prose, he had heard the stories so many times that pictures of his own had formed in his mind with the exactness and relentless tenacity of a home movie. And while he had seen most of them anyway, the films of the twentieth century had been summarily dismissed and forbidden by his family. All lies, they had said—the worst kind of Hollywood butchery, savage propaganda, an insult to the race and to their ancestors. And Victor agreed. He saw them out of curiosity. He had to know for himself. None of these other images, comical and sad, were powerful enough to displace the images he had formed in his own mind, though: people who had been constructed, yes, from parts harvested from the dead, but who were nevertheless beautiful, noble, and miraculous. Frightening? Only to those who had no appreciation for the art or who were unable to wrap their minds around the science or who were moralistic and cried sacrilege or who became unfortunate victims of Great-Granddad's rage. This was Victor's view of things, passed on to him from his mother and father, his aunts and uncles, and in large part from the woman he loved more than Mrs. Terhart and possibly more than his own mother: Grandma Elizabeth, who, while keeping the memories of the family alive and intact, was the person most responsible for the end of the art of making monsters.

In his bedroom, still sulking and smarting a little from the realization that he could not be open about his family's history just as he was becoming familiar enough with it and proud enough of it to actually discuss it, Grandma Elizabeth's voice came through his closed bedroom door. "Can I come in?" His parents were out of the house, and he was alone with Grandma. Without Victor's awareness, on that evening, Grandma Elizabeth was there by design for purposes other than to simply watch Victor while Mom and Dad were out. She had come to him with a gift.

She came into the room in her graceful, deliberate way, sat down next to him on his bed, and handed him the present.

"What is it, Grandma Elizabeth?"

"Feel it. Feel the package. Can you guess?"

"Yes, but I won't guess, Grandma. I want it to be a surprise."

"Let's not waste another minute. Open it, Victor."

Elizabeth had prepared herself to be disappointed. She was giving him a book that he would not be able to read until he was perhaps twice his present age—and even then with limited understanding—but Victor was thrilled to receive it. Elizabeth was pleased beyond all measure. The expression on her face made it seem as though the sun was shining on it.

Indoors, at night, she lit up like a lamp. And Victor would never forget this moment.

"This is the story of the very beginning, Victor—the beginning of your family."

"*Frankenstein.*" He recognized the word immediately.

"Yes, but I want to tell you the rest. I want you to know the rest. And I hope you will remember. I know you are young, but I am very, very old. And I will not be here very much longer."

"Where are you going, Grandma?"

"I will die soon, Victor."

"What does that mean?"

"It means—it means that I will no longer continue in this shape and form."

"Will you become light, Grandma Elizabeth?"

"Yes. I will become light."

By degrees and over time, Victor learned the story from Grandma Elizabeth, and later, but much sooner than anyone could imagine, the rest would fall into place. And as Victor knew he was meant to do, even as a second grader, somehow, someday, he would finish the story.

Of Bedtime Stories

Whenever Grandma Elizabeth visited from that point on, she made a ritual of tucking Victor into bed, and, as she told her daughter she would do, she "read" to him. Actually, she was presenting to Victor what would become known famously as the monster talk, telling Victor stories of the family's history. He would be able to read the story from Shelley when he grew older and smarter, yes, but mostly, and from memory, Grandma Elizabeth would speak of what happened after that story ended.

"My father, your great-granddad," she said on one of the first of these occasions, "was a genius. He was a little troubled from his experiences in Europe, but he was a great scientist, a linguist, a poet, a first-rate gardener and hunter, and a master builder. But he was very lonely. Instead of lying down to die, though, he had to experience what was always just out of his reach. So his desire to build a companion, someone to love, made the study of science the most important thing in the world to him, and before he moved to this country, he learned everything there was to know about his creator's art. And it came easy to him."

And Elizabeth went on to tell Victor about how his great-grandfather worked tirelessly and secretly for years in libraries and laboratories across Europe. He was fortunate in finding "donors" for everything he needed. "He called them donors," Elizabeth said, "so that he wouldn't feel so bad about the work he was doing."

"Why would he feel bad, Grandma?"

"Well, dear, because he was digging up graves and stealing dead bodies. And that's not very nice behavior in polite society."

"Oh." Victor was wide-eyed.

And Elizabeth continued. "Everything was going right for him, as if the universe was falling perfectly into place. He thought to himself, 'If it comes so easy, how could it be wrong?' So your great-granddaddy, he built himself the wife his creator refused to build."

"Wow," Victor said and closed his eyes.

Sometimes she kept talking even when she could not tell whether or not he was still with her. "I understand," she said, "that the awakening was a phenomenal thing to witness and experience—a throbbing, pulsating, gyrating, euphoric, galvanizing sensation that swirled through the veins and organs of both creator and created alike.

"Are you listening, sweetie?" She was happy to see that he had nodded off and was sound asleep.

The next time she was over for the weekly family dinner, Victor insisted that Grandma Elizabeth tuck him in. "Tell me about your mother," Victor said, and Elizabeth laughed for some mysterious reason.

"Yes, Victor. I will tell you that my mother was a beautiful monster, and Daddy loved her with every fiber of his being. And she came together easily, almost seamlessly, except for one tiny little problem. He used a rib. And he wasn't trying to be funny. It was a fact that this particular donor was missing a rib in a really important way, and he could not stand to see his wife shorted in this manner. He busted a gut, Victor, and gave up a rib. So we children referred to our parents as Adam and Eve!"

"I don't get it, Grandma. What does that have to do with Adam and Eve?"

"The Bible story, Victor, says that God created Eve from one of Adam's ribs."

"Is that a true story?"

"No, dear, that is what we call mythology. Some people believe it's literally true. And those people are very silly. Shall we continue?"

"Yes!" He was very excited, and Grandma worried only a little bit that tonight's story would have to be a long one.

"My father, remember, had no name, and so he didn't really name my mother. He preferred instead the use of pet names. His first words to her, after the awakening, were simply 'Bonjour, ma cherie.'"

Victor laughed.

"And from then on, for nearly a century, he continued to refer to her either as "my dear" or "my love," and she responded in kind. But we were not so brave as to call our parents Adam and Eve to their faces. We only joked about it with them once or twice in the whole of our existence together, kept the joke mostly to ourselves, and continued in the normal way to call them Papa and Mama. Mother was kind and caring and strong, and she was also smart as a whip. She learned to read—or relearned to read in her new life—with some of the greatest books of all time. And these are the books that we learned from: the Bible, *Paradise Lost*, *Faust*, Dante's *Inferno*."

"Will you read those to me?"

"They're pretty tough, Victor. But we can try sometime."

"Okay, so tell me how they got here, Grandma. How'd we get to America?"

These two lovers, Elizabeth told Victor, the monster and his new monster-bride, stowed away on an eighteenth-century war vessel headed for Boston as if they were booking a pleasure cruise. It was that easy. Elizabeth thought, but she was not sure, that somehow Adam had come by a great deal of money that he must have used to pay their way over. And when they arrived in the New World, they knew instinctively to travel quickly and stealthily due west, a hundred years before it would become fashionable to do so. They beat Lewis and Clark to the punch, pre-paved the Oregon Trail for the Expedition, and then turned sharply southward through California and into the dessert. And, being strong and resourceful and no strangers to adversity natural or unnatural (weather, difficult terrain, hostile natives, guilt, fear), nothing could stop them. They traveled, mostly on foot, thousands of miles across the continent and settled finally in Arizona. They quickly adapted to and then learned to love the heat of the place, the red rock, the dessert sand, the strange, otherworldly creatures, and the ever-present company of the sun and the stars.

"Grandma," Victor said, "how come you're so old?"

"Victor, that's no way to speak to your elders."

"No, you know what I mean. I mean, you're old. Really old. And so is Mama. It's like you're way older than most old people."

She knew what he was after. "For some reason, Victor, our species, our kind of people, are remarkably robust—I mean, we're really strong, built to last, as they say.

Adam and Eve both lived 150 years. And us children have had long lives. If we're lucky and something else doesn't come around and kill us, we keep going until we are very old indeed. We're a hearty, healthy brood. For some mysterious reason, we don't get diseases, and we don't wrinkle up like prunes. At 150, our daddy looked very much like he did the moment he wandered out into the world for the first time in Ingolstadt. Victor, we don't know why a creature created from parts of dead people would not have a rougher start to begin with. We don't know why the jumbled genetics from all of the various donors wouldn't cause certain problems in the development of the offspring. Did Dr. Frankenstein, and then later your great-grandfather, know hundreds of years ahead of his time something about the genetic imprint that triggers the aging process? Was the family line simply blessed somehow? We just don't know, Victor. There are people in the Bible stories who lived nearly a thousand years—but I think that's hogwash. Maybe, just maybe, some of those people were likewise endowed and lived 200 years and then Moses or whoever was writing those books just exaggerated a little bit. Hey, Victor, maybe they were monsters!" She decided to end this evening's monster talk on a light note, gave her knees a double pat with her hands as a signal, and reached over and affectionately tousled the boy's hair. "Good night, Victor."

"No, keep going. Keep going. I'm not tired. Grandma Elizabeth, tell me about the other monsters."

"Well, then, okay. But first I have to talk about a very mature subject matter."

"Grandma, duh. What, do you think I'm a kindergartener or something?"

"Your great-grandparents believed they would live and die together, alone. Neither of them believed in the idea that the world must be peopled—or monstered, as would be their case. For as smart as they both were, they were totally ignorant about sex and about what consequences it could create in their lives."

"I've heard about that sex word. Tell me about it."

Even Grandma Elizabeth, a bold woman not easily offended or shocked, began to blush in the presence of an audience so young, but she charged ahead. "Adam and Eve discovered it accidentally, on an especially cold evening, huddled together in a shelter in the wilderness. Their bodies came together and connected in this very unusual but pleasurable way. Three months later, Eve was fat, and six months after that, she gave birth to William the Second in 1750, two years later to Ernest the Second, and remarkably, 107 years later, in 1857, to Elizabeth, that's me, also the Second."

"Okay," Victor said, but he could tell she was avoiding something. He tried to figure out exactly what that was—something to do with the sex word, perhaps—but the earlier, more relevant question to him still had no answer. "You said you would tell me about the monsters. You are the daughter of monsters, and you are not a monster. I am the great-grandson of monsters, and I am not a monster. How come there were more monsters?"

"Adam and Eve would have been content to live out the rest of their lives together as a family, without complicating things further by spreading out the family line. It was Adam's sons, William and Ernest, insistent on companionship as your grandfather was, that convinced him to go back into the library and then into the laboratory to produce suitable mates. Adam, remember, was no dummy, and he knew from studying closely various European family lines and learning about the dangers of inbreeding, that to ask his first born male to mate with his first born female would be a big mistake—it would be wrong. Thank God for that. For the longest time, we remained in isolation. We did not mingle with any of our neighbors. So to solve the problem, he did for his two sons—and then much, much later tried to do for me—exactly what he did for himself. He created a monster. He built two women, and then a man, as mates for his children."

Victor was sleeping again. Elizabeth turned off his bedside lamp, stood up, and crept quietly out of the room, closing the door behind her.

"Do you remember, Victor, what we spoke about last time?"

"The boys, William and Ernest, wanted sex with girls, and Granddad didn't like it, so he made monsters for them."

"Almost, Victor. It wasn't just about sex, but love, companionship."

"Oh. And then I remember I wanted to know why monster babies don't look like monsters."

"As far as I know, there has never been a monster baby, only adults. By physical appearances, William and Ernest and myself were normal in every way. Look at me—aren't I a beauty?"

"Yes, Grandma." Victor blushed and giggled, covering his face with the blankets and sheets.

"Adam and Eve were flabbergasted by how beautiful their progeny were."

"Flabber what? Progeny who?"

"We children were beautiful. Adam and Eve were surprised. In some strange way, they half-expected their boys to be born with stitches, looking pieced together and ugly like their parents. But as young men, and then as adults, my brothers would have been serious catch to women in society in this eighteenth- and nineteenth-century America—if they cleaned up proper and acquired a nice suit of clothes. But our parents had convinced them that to mingle with the humans would prove disastrous and might ultimately lead to the end of their existence on this earth. And they, of course, especially Adam, had terrifying stories from their own experiences as proof of their warnings. William and Ernest had no problem believing these tales, but that didn't change the basic facts of the situation: They wanted companions for life. They wanted mates. And because they were raised by monsters, they had no particular aversion to monsters. These boys were not easily shocked or frightened, and so they became accustomed to their new mates in relatively short order.

"And Daddy went on and on about the art and how wonderful it was, mostly for my benefit, because—I'll tell you a secret, Victor—I did not want a monster husband. But he would rant and rave, scream and shout, like one of these Baptist ministers. He'd say, 'do you know, children, what it is like to be *born?* Do you know what it's like to *awaken?* Oh, it is a glorious thing.'" Victor began to giggle. Elizabeth was in a kind of state that he had never seen before. It was almost like she was on television. She had forgotten about his presence and was momentarily possessed by the spirit of her father, bouncing up and down on the bed as she spoke, which was kind of fun for Victor, but also a little spooky.

"'Think about it,' Papa would say. 'You come into the world fully conscious of self. You are not an infant. Your mind is mature. Yes, you have forgotten who you used to be. In my case, I could not speak. William, your wife was fully linguistic, and when she opened her eyes, she thanked me! She smiled. She was not in pain. And Ernest, you remember teaching your lovely wife to move more gracefully. She was awkward, oh boy, but she improved quickly and was spirited, never despondent. There is, generally, a disoriented state for quite awhile, but throughout there is a kind of vibrancy that most human beings will never know. When they do know it, they call it *enthusiasm*. Do you know what enthusiasm means, boys and girls?'" Victor did not know if he should speak, but he shook his head, because he did not know what enthusiasm meant. "'It means to be filled with God. It is glorious. See, I suffered unduly for the sloppiness of my creator. He was not only sloppy, but ambivalent. He was not sure whether he was doing evil or good. He became obsessed. His game was off. He didn't name me, he abandoned me, he ran from me, and he died with most of his secrets. And I suffered. I suffered a long time so that your mother, your wives, and soon, Elizabeth, your husband, wouldn't have to.'" Suddenly, Elizabeth was still.

"Are you okay, Grandma?"

"Phew. I got carried away there a little bit, Victor. I hope I didn't scare you."

"Only a little," he said.

Weeks later, Victor asked Grandma Elizabeth, "Why didn't you want your daddy to make you a monster?"

"Victor, I had started to travel around and I met some people and I fancied a few different men and I did not need Daddy to create something for me that was already there if I just reached out and grabbed for it."

"I think it would be fun to have your own monster. As long as he was nice."

"But would you want to kiss one?"

"I don't think that would be fun."

"And on top of it all, Victor, I had come to believe that monster-making was wrong. My daddy told me that I didn't know what I was talking about, that I didn't understand or appreciate the power and gift of the awakening. And I told him, I said, '*You* don't understand the power and gift of being human.' I said I thought all three of us had been blessed, equally blessed with another kind of awakening. We came into this world dependent and stupid, but we were loved, and we learned and grew and struggled. We worked harder for every benefit available to us during our development, and the rewards are sweeter because of it. But your great-grandfather would have none of it. And finally, he was growing too old for the work and a bit feeble-minded. So much unlike his creator in many ways, toward the end he nevertheless took on one of Dr. Frankenstein's most serious faults and gifts: he could not be stopped. But neither could I be stopped. And while Daddy was making a monster, his daughter was looking for love."

"Yuck," Victor said.

The monster the monster built, as Elizabeth put it to Victor, was prodigiously articulate but very hideous to look at. He was, above all the other monsters, the most obviously constructed from spare parts, and none of those parts were in harmony with the others. The nose was too big for the eyes, belonging, as it did, to a dead giant, while the eyes were harvested from a deceased dwarf. The ears did not match, clearly from two different "donors." The mouth was a patchwork of curls and snarls, and the teeth were torturously crooked. It was the first constructed face Adam had attempted, and he chose this particular road because he had come by the head of an imminent and promising scholar who had had a most unfortunate accident, causing not only his death, but also the destruction of most of his facial features and sense organs. But here was a brain that the most heinous-looking creature on the planet would be proud to call his own. The mind of a philosopher. The precision of a great mathematician. The inner vision of a poet. The body of a brute. A monster no woman could love. Why Adam did not simply find another head for the brain remains a mystery.

And Elizabeth said to Victor, in the last of her bedtime stories, last because she thought of it as the end of the narrative, "I told your grandfather that I would not marry a monster! But he had already made the monster, Victor. I told him it was the worst thing he could have done. I told him it was a sin. I told him marrying his monster would just make the sin bigger. I told him I could never love a monster that wasn't my own Daddy. He said, 'Is it because he is so ugly?' And I said, 'If it were only that simple. But now that you mention it,' I said, 'he is most hideous. It is terrible enough to look at him. I can barely imagine holding him, kissing him, or loving him without a great queasiness in my stomach. You can't wish this for me, Daddy!' I knew a bit of the world, Victor. I was young and beautiful, and I knew there were human beings out there, a whole host of beautiful humans, beautiful men, who would love me."

"Yuck," Victor said.

So Elizabeth the Second, Victor's grandmother, broke the mold. She would not marry a monster. She would not make love to a monster. She would not bear a monster's child. So she was the first one, early in the lineage, to crossbreed, and from that moment forward, there would be no more monsters made. The line was now, in Victor's age, at the end of the twentieth century and into the twenty-first, completely human. The making of monsters was a dead art. There were no living monsters left in the family, or, as far as anyone knew, alive in the world.

And that was the end of Victor's bedtime story.

Of Namesakes, First Love, and a Nightmare

Victor liked his name—his first name. He liked the way it sounded; the fact that here, in the southwest United States of America, it was an unusual name for a white boy; and that, for all intents and purposes, as names can do, it seemed to fit him nicely. The irony was not lost on him, though, as he grew older and could appreciate it. It would be like a Christian woman naming her first-born Jesus, or more like God, or a Buddhist woman naming her child Buddha. Imagine the audacity. Maybe that was another thing he liked about it: its aplomb, its potency, its evocative qualities. It was a container for all of his family's history. Unlike Jesus or God, though, Victor's namesake was no benevolent deity or saint, was fallible, was in many ways more a monster than his monster, and failed at many things—in fact, at all things, save for the one thing that made Victor's existence possible. He failed as a student, as a son, as a brother, as a friend, as a husband, and most notably as a father. But all of these failures paved Victor's way into the world, and Dr. Frankenstein of the eighteenth century was eventually forgiven.

Of course, Adam would have been the only one alive who had been "wronged" by the creator of this most remarkable family, and he would hold on to most of that grudge until he died. But at the time of Adam's procreation, tribute was finally paid to the doctor through the naming of Adam's offspring, a tradition his sons and daughters and their sons and daughters would continue all the way into the end of the twentieth century.

William, Ernest, Elizabeth, Justine, and Henry: all were names of people from the original story, loved ones of Frankenstein, Adam's hapless victims. He could give them life again. And ever afterward, the mad scientist would be venerated, almost worshipped by Adam's lineage. And why not? Could a person possibly hate his own source? Does the river hate the mountain or the ocean? Do the trees hate the air and the sun or the earth? Yes, children sometimes hate their parents, but human beings are unique in this, aren't they? It's a sickness, albeit an understandable one. Adam hated the doctor, and it was mostly spite that kept him going—but it was spite against the doctor that gave him this remarkable capacity to love his own children. Good comes from bad and bad from good, an almost elementary truth that human beings still, most of them, have great difficulty accepting. "Some good will come of this." This was something Grandma Elizabeth said often—and half a dozen times to Victor specifically.

One day in the second grade, there were a great number of children on the playground doing the arthritic zombie walk across Victor's path, pretending—inaccurately, of course—to be Frankenstein. It was a strange sensation for him, seeing them do this, seeing it catch on, fad-like, increasing in frequency to the point where almost every day he'd see at least two kids try to pull it off. Victor was at once hurt and entertained. The hurtful part of it was, of course, that he knew that the intention was to get a laugh from other kids at his expense, and that ultimately, the laughs would come because his feelings were hurt. And this was the dominant response in Victor for quite a while: a dejectedness, a spurned feeling—the idea that he was hated. But then there was another part of him, trying to insist its way into Victor's consciousness, that knew most of these kids were not worth knowing, were ridiculous and sad, and were, truly, inferior to him. He wanted to laugh back, but the hurt he was feeling usually had the upper hand. Then, on that day, something happened. He felt himself on the verge of tears as one boy, especially skilled in the zombie walk, got a number of kids to laugh at once, a whole pack of them. Victor looked up at the zombie boy and over at the pack of laughing kids, some of them pointing at zombie boy, others pointing at Victor, when he saw another kid standing apart from the crowd, laughing not at zombie boy or at him, but laughing at the kids who were laughing. And then he did something else: he looked directly at Victor and smiled in a conspiratorial kind of way, as if to say "Look at them. They're idiots." Victor felt himself shift inside, and before the first tear fell, he was laughing.

The boy approached. A dark-haired, cherub-faced boy, taller than Victor by half a head, came up, put his arm under and around Victor's arm, turned Victor from the crowd of heckling children, and escorted him away by the arm like Victor had seen his father escort his mother or Grandma Elizabeth. This new boy started talking right away.

"I bet you your great-granddaddy doesn't look anything like that when he walks."

"My great-granddaddy is dead."

"Don't pay any attention to them. They are only jealous they don't have monsters in their families."

"What's your name?" Victor asked.

"My name is Dennis, and I am a big fan of your great-granddad's. But I realize that I don't know anything about him. I know what those kids know about the fake ones in movies. Have you seen those movies?"

"Some."

"I'd really like to know about the real Frankenstein. Would you be my friend?"

"I don't know."

"Well, I'll let you think about it for a while. But I can't wait forever, you know."

"Okay, I've thought about it," Victor said, impulsively. He hadn't thought about it at all, but he had a sense about this Dennis person, a strong sense, and it was a good feeling that he immediately trusted. "I'll be your friend."

Dennis was Victor's first love—a friend that captured his heart like no other person his age ever had or would again for a very long time. A strange sadness and longing accompanied every absence, and the absences were many, because Dennis lived relatively far away and was a third grader. They saw each other at school on the playground for the thirty minutes of recess, and they spent every minute of that time together. Victor, in his childlike way, told Dennis all he could think of regarding his interesting pedigree. He told him about the original story from Shelley as best as he could, remarking mostly that his great-granddaddy's name, contrary to what all of these stupid kids on the playground insisted, was not Frankenstein after all, that he had no name, that he was not a retard and did not walk like one, that he was treated horribly by everybody except for the blind man, and that he came to regret the ugly things he did in his quest for revenge against the doctor. And then he continued the story from the polar ice caps: Granddad's trip back to Europe to create his bride, the emigration to America, and the efforts to raise a family. And it was remarkable to Victor how Dennis listened and asked questions but never seemed to doubt any of what Victor told him.

When apart from Dennis, Victor was bereft. Now, in time, as soon as he discovered girls, he would repress these memories, but later they would come back to him in vivid emotional detail as the losses piled up—as the first losses as a young adult reminded him of those he had forgotten from his childhood. There was no sexual interest in Dennis as far as he would be able to remember; Victor did not understand sex this early and could not concern himself too deeply with what Grandma Elizabeth had told him about monster sexuality. It was just a melting in the heart, a gladness in Dennis's presence, an extreme sense of longing in his absence, and a sadness to the point of tears when he thought, morbidly, in bed at night about how his friend might be lost to him. These were the feelings about one's own gender that one learns very quickly to discard growing up.

Months after their first acquaintance, when their solidarity had gone a long way to quell the teasing from other kids, their stories had been told, and their friendship had solidified, Dennis announced the news on the recess playground. "Mom says I'm old enough now to have a friend stay over. Come to my house. We can stay up and watch scary movies. Can you come?"

Victor did not know if he could come but was thrilled at the invitation and immediately got permission from Justine. The date was set for the next weekend. Justine had talked to Dennis's mom. Everything seemed okay, but there was this conversation between Victor and his mother on the eve of the stay-over.

Justine implored, "Victor, please do not talk to Dennis's mother about the family."

"But Dennis already knows everything, Mother, and he may have told. I didn't tell him not to."

"Jesus Christ," was all that Justine could think to say.

But as Justine dropped him off at Dennis's apartment doorstep the next afternoon, Victor made a promise that if Dennis's mother didn't know already everything there was to know, he would not take pains to tell her.

Justine was about one hundred and twenty-five years old but didn't look a day over forty-five. Given this kind of longevity, the members of her family had to get used to certain unavoidable facts: One, barring any kind of freak fatal accident, they would always outlive their spouses. Two, once they arrived at a physical appearance approximating the middle age of our typical human adult, they would visibly stop aging, freezing somewhere between thirty-five and fifty. Three, unless they were content to live very much alone or confined to the companionship of family members likewise endowed, they would probably want to partner up again. Justine's first husband died in 1970. He had a heart attack in his sleep at the ripe old age of seventy-five. Justine, looking and feeling every bit like a spry thirty-eight, remarried in 1989 and a year later gave birth to Victor.

As she drove away from Dennis's house, she worried about what might come up and how Victor might be mortified once again by the disbelief and reproach of another adult. And she thought of her own troubles around this very thing and how almost a decade ago, as a woman of 112 years, it seemed so impossible to find a date, let alone a husband, who would first of all believe the damn story and second of all fall in love with a woman sixty-five years his senior. Justine was tired of juggling with numbers and had really stopped counting a long time ago. But she valued the truth and didn't want a partner with whom she could not be truthful. Telling the truth was hard; in many avenues of her life, she had to lie. All through childhood and her adolescence she lied or at the very least withheld a great deal. Every time she began a new job or started a new career, she had to lie. Coming into the department store business twenty years ago, she had said in her application materials that she was thirty-five. She was thirty-eight only a few years back when she applied for a position in management of women's apparel. Her supervisors, co-workers and employees—none of them knew or had ever known her real age—were absolutely baffled as to how she kept up her good looks. But Justine knew, even though she felt good, healthy as an ox or a monster, that she didn't have very much longer to live—unless she had her mother Elizabeth's good fortune. *My god*, she thought, *that woman will live forever*. But she knew better. They were as mortal as any human being. They just had all been gifted with more time to play, to experiment, with this life.

And Elizabeth was a great experimenter. Justine always joked inwardly that her mother should have embraced monster-making; she would have been a pro. But she invested her prodigious creativity into other endeavors, and while she was inflexible about the immorality of creating life from death, she was absolutely insistent about making life from life. Justine envied her mother that. It was an attribute that did not effectively rub off on her.

Victor had never seen this television show called the *X-Files*, but Dennis was a true enthusiast and recorded each week's episode with his VCR. Much of the evening was spent in front of the TV watching these shows, episode after episode, fast-forwarding through the commercials, and watching the especially yucky parts again and again. There was the one about the forest bugs that Victor liked. He was upset by the sewer monster episode. And he could barely keep his eyes open during the episode about a family of inbreeds who kept their legless and armless mommy under the floorboards. Dennis's mother asked him if he had seen shows like this before, and Victor lied about it and tried to act brave. One thing, oddly enough, that gave him courage throughout was this beautiful FBI woman. He could not take his eyes off of her when she was in a scene. She made him want to weep, and he didn't understand why. He longed to see more of her, but Dennis insisted that they move on to the feature, a classic: the Boris Karloff *Frankenstein.* And Victor felt so much like the authority. With great pride and apparent learning, he pointed out all of the inaccuracies. The original story still too difficult for him to read, he reported to Dennis and his mother all of what he had been told by Grandma Elizabeth. There was no Henry Clerval, Frankenstein's great friend, in this film. Victor wasn't even a Victor, but a Henry—but not the right Henry. They invented this stupid assistant character. No Justine. No blind man. And of course, this is where the ideas originated that the monster hated fire, was only capable of grunts and moans, was chased down by an angry mob, and was then burned alive inside of a windmill. A windmill! Victor went on and on and then suddenly remembered what his mother had told him. He was mortified. But when he looked at Dennis's mom over there, sitting on the couch, she didn't appear to be perplexed or upset. She was wearing a nightgown, but her legs were bare below the knee. Her naked feet were tucked up underneath her, and she was smiling. She was impressed. She had not caught on that he was speaking about events he believed had actually happened centuries ago, but rather thought he was being a kind of bookworm's boy, incensed already at the liberties Hollywood had taken and would continue to take with great works of literature. His secret was safe, and Dennis had not said a word. He wanted to tell Dennis that he loved him. He thought of it and immediately felt a tear form in his eye. He thought better of it, though, and grabbed a handful of popcorn from the bowl on the coffee table.

The lights were out, and Victor was in a strange bed in a strange room, fast asleep. It went something like this. Victor was being chased by a monster on a tricycle. But first, he was held in a vice of some kind that immobilized his entire body, and he was forced by the implementation of this machine to look upon the thing as it stood before him. The arms were barely operable, most of the time hanging willy-nilly on either side of a convoluted, arthritic torso. The legs were mismatched, one horribly shorter than the other. The face was unrecognizable as a face, wet with mucus and tears, the sense organs all misplaced around the head: ears where a mouth should be, two mouths where eyes would go, eyes like those of a fish on either side of its head, and teeth protruding like horns through its skin. The monster straddled a tricycle. When the vice let Victor loose, he turned to run, and as he ran, the monster sped after him on his trike.

This is how it was according to Dennis, because Victor could not remember a stitch of it. In the middle of the night—or, more accurately, very early in the morning—Victor woke up screaming bloody murder, evidently from the aforementioned nightmare. Victor did not remember. He had no memory of Dennis's panic to help him, thinking Victor might be sick or having a seizure or dying, frightening himself halfway out of his child mind, and screaming for the help of his mother. Victor had no memory of this woman trying to calm him down, a child that was not hers, fearful that some terrible thing could have befallen him away from home and shaking him awake, trying to stay calm and not to be angry. And because Victor could not remember, he was exceedingly puzzled the next morning as Dennis and his mom sat at the breakfast table in complete silence, an embarrassed, mysterious stillness. Victor could not help but be self-conscious.

"What's the matter?" he finally asked.

"You had a nightmare," Dennis said. And that, for the time being, anyway, was the end of it.

Justine assumed the scary movies were to blame. They were not a television family, and Victor was not used to such images. But Victor knew better. Grandma Elizabeth knew better. The sewer man and the inbred family may have been a kind of springboard, but Victor's night terrors originated in reality—or in Elizabeth's version of it, at least. Of the stories swimming around in Victor's memory, most were relatively innocuous, and some were downright homey. But one haunted Victor and visited him with some frequency in his nightmares, imbued as it was with his grandmother's fierce stance against the power of reanimating the dead: the story of the monster that got away. It was the final proof, Elizabeth had said, of the problem inherent in this black science. There was no way Adam could escape the fact that, as long as he pursued the art of monster making, sooner or later he was doomed to recreate his own creator's mistakes. He could not leave well enough alone, and despite Elizabeth's protests, as you know, her monster husband was made, was rejected, and fled into the world, deformities and all, never to be seen again.

It was the only time Elizabeth could remember her father speaking in anger, but this was rage—pure, unadulterated rage.

"What happened, Elizabeth?" He scowled at her. He was seven feet tall to her five foot six, and he loomed, casting a shadow over her world.

"I told him that I could not love him. That he was a mistake."

"You told him he was a mistake?"

"You're scaring me, Father!"

"You whore," he said, and he was weeping. "Did you tell him about your love-making with the humans? Did you tell him of your prostitution?"

The words were like blows. She could not breathe. "Father, you don't know what you're saying."

"I know you. I know you." And he stormed away. Adam searched the desert and all of the surrounding towns tirelessly for his lost creation. The son-in-law his daughter would not have as her husband would suffer the same fate he had suffered—the fate Adam had promised himself and God that no other monster would ever have to suffer again. It brought everything back to him: the desperation he felt in Ingolstadt, the confusion, the bitterness, the soul-eating hatred that would have made him capable of killing a child. *That's what I have given this new creation*, he thought. *This is what I have unleashed upon the earth.*

Adam was missing for two weeks, and when he returned, he said, cryptically and without elaboration, that the new monster was dead. And he, too, slowly but certainly, began to die.

And even though Justine did not immediately see the most probable cause of Victor's nightmares, she had heard Elizabeth tell these stories to Victor and had seen Victor's eyes ablaze with awe. "You're scaring him, Mother, with those freak tales."

"Who's the freak in these tales, I wonder?"

"Stop it. Those stories about your monster husband. They scare him."

"Perhaps," she said.

"I wish you'd stop."

"Some good will come from this."

"Jesus Christ," Justine said.

A few days after the sleepover, noticing a new and disturbing distance between him and Dennis, feeling a kind of anxiety he had never known, his entire little body shaking, he found the courage to ask Dennis if they could watch scary movies together again someday. Dennis's mother didn't want Victor over again, he was told. "You scared her really bad." Dennis was fighting back tears.

"I don't understand," Victor said. "I don't remember." Victor felt desperation welling up inside of him, and he said what seemed at the time to be a very strange thing: "Please don't leave me."

It was unrelated completely—but because Victor could not know this, he suffered immeasurably when he learned a week later that Dennis and his mother would be moving to another state. He would probably never see either one of them again.

Of Recess, Boys and Girls, and Something Inside

Victor was lost on the recess playground for quite some time. He walked with his head down and his eyes diverted or sat alone on a bench at the corner of the field. Other children would fly by in every direction, making their noise and playing their games. Sometimes he'd be underneath the bleachers covered in shadow, deep in thought about Dennis's final departure and full of trepidation about his own culpability. He felt utterly abandoned. But he did not blame Dennis. He assumed that his mother had given him no choice in the matter, that she had said simply, "Dennis, we're moving away from that terrible boy." And what choice did children have?

Emerging from under the bleachers and walking almost invisibly through crowds of small people, he eventually stopped looking at his shoes. His head straightened up, his eyes opened wide, and he began to watch and listen. Victor watched and was ignored. He imagined he was doing some kind of work, always on the periphery, observing. There was something scientific about it, he thought, and while he was not sure about what he was looking for or why he was looking, he appeared to be engaged in some kind of serious ethnographic study. Making a permanent record in his brain and filing it under a gigantic imaginary question mark, this is what he noticed: The boys and the girls stayed away from each other, mostly.

Boys were always hitting each other or throwing balls at one another. The boys did a lot of running, too. Most of the running appeared aimless. He watched two boys run in a circle for about five minutes until they were exhausted and fell down on the pavement. Boys would take things from each other and run away. They would break each other's toys and laugh while running. The girls, however, were talking, skipping rope, playing hopscotch or tetherball, and always laughing. Sometimes they would sing. Rarely did they run. Victor preferred to watch the girls.

Victor noticed that the only time boys and girls played together was when they were in love. He knew they were in love because he had overheard them saying so. But on the playground, they were unbelievably nasty to one another. If a boy loved a girl, he would push her into the dirt. If a girl loved a boy, she would put sawdust down his shirt and pants. They would call each other names. Uglyhead. Fatso. Stinkbreath. Dorkface. Fartknocker. The girls would chase the boys (the only time he ever saw them run) endlessly around the field, or the boys would chase the girls endlessly around the field. Victor noticed that the ones who loved each other the most, or professed they did, inflicted the most pain on one another. So if a boy really loved a girl, she would know because, at the end of one of their exchanges, either because her feelings were hurt or because of some physical injury, she was crying. And if a girl really loved a boy, he would know by the pain in his butt, the splinters in his underwear, the bruise on his shin, or the anger in his heart. Invariably, both boys and girls would verbally express their love for one another by crying at the top of their lungs all the way across the playground, "I hate you!"

It made absolutely no sense to Victor. He loved Dennis and would never hit him, curse at him, or push him into the dirt. He suffered intensely and shuddered visibly, sitting alone on his bench and trying to imagine Dennis pulling sawdust splinters out of his knees. It was wrong. "I'm sorry, Dennis," he said out loud to no one, apologizing for his imaginary sins. He could not derive any pleasure from this fantasy. He thought maybe there was something he did not understand, that he was missing some key element in the rituals of love: maybe, he thought, if he was mean to others, they would be nicer to him.

And one day, as he was approached by a pack of zombie boys for the first time in perhaps a month or two, he tried to imagine that these kids, instead of demonstrating their hatred for him, might in fact be showing their affection instead.

"Hey, Frankenbaby," said Jimmy, a raggedy little child who always smelled like gasoline. There were perhaps four or five boys behind him, laughing already.

"Hello," said Victor.

"Do you miss your boyfriend?"

The children behind Jimmy were unexpectedly quiet. The anticipation was palpable; it was as if they were holding their breath. Victor was confused. The question was innocuous enough. "Yes," he said. "I do." And the pack of zombie kids erupted in hideous, almost demonic laughter. And suddenly they were doing a dance around him. Victor was encircled, and the names started flying: Monsterboy, Frankenbaby, Frankenfurter, Frankenfuck—and especially popular, a word that caused Victor no end of puzzlement: Frankenfaggot. *They like me*, Victor was saying over and over inside his head, smiling at them but feeling all the while like someone was pulling his heart through his chest with a pair of rusty salad tongs.

After school, Mrs. Terhart sat behind her desk taking deep breaths and closing her eyes. It was quiet. She loved the quiet classroom that book-ended her workday. She tried every day, as the schedule of meetings and committees and conferences allowed, to spend ten minutes in the morning, and another ten minutes in the afternoon, sitting in silence behind her desk. Eyes closed and breathing, despite the open window not three feet from where she sat, she could smell the crayons and the paper and the glue, a hint of milk and graham cracker, and a tinge of gasoline. *Damn*, she thought, *why do they let that boy play around in the garage?* And then she heard a sound like footsteps and then like breathing—but it was not her breathing.

"Are you sleeping, Mrs. Terhart?"

At first she was unsure that the voice did not come from within her own mind, even though she knew immediately whose voice it was. She opened her eyes.

"Hello, Victor. What are you doing? Did you miss the bus?"

"No, Mrs. Terhart. Mom will pick me up soon."

"Well, what's up, then, my friend?"

"Mrs. Terhart, what's a faggot?"

"Well, Victor," she said. She looked up at the ceiling and sighed. She remained calm and quiet but not without some significant inner effort. This was a new one for the second grade. Every year, it seemed, there was some new intrusion on the innocence of childhood, earlier and earlier—an awareness of things of which children should not have to be aware. Maybe, she thought, she could protect him from this one somehow. And she decided to lie, but as soon as the words were out, she was angry with herself. "It's a bundle of sticks, Victor."

She could see it in his eyes that he was not satisfied with that response.

"Why would kids be calling me a bundle of sticks?" he said.

"Oh, dear." She was embarrassed, but she could tell that Victor had forgiven the lie already. Suddenly, she felt protective and angry. "Who's calling you that, Victor?"

"It doesn't matter. I just want to know what it means."

"Who called you that?"

"No."

"Victor, I think you are too young. Let's just say that it's a very mean word to use. A stupid, hurtful thing to say. People who use that language are stupid, fearful people, and you should pay no attention to them."

He had never really seen her angry before. It frightened him a little, and he thought he might be the cause of that anger. But he had to know. "Tell me what it means, Mrs. Terhart."

"It's horrible," she went on, more to herself than to Victor. The indignation swirled inside her mind against the carelessness of parents and older siblings who would expose the children in their families to such ugliness, equipping them with the tools of hatred. Damn them all.

Victor could see her thinking, could see her fuming, but he forged on.

"Tell me what it means."

"It is a mean, bigoted, nasty word people use against boys who love boys."

"Then I am a faggot," Victor said without any misgiving, as if proud of finding some kind of label to attach to himself.

"No, Victor, you are not."

"But I am. I love Dennis."

"The love you have for your friends is a different kind of love. There is friendly love, family love, and then there is romantic love."

"How do you know the difference?"

"You will know, Victor, In time you will know. Romantic love makes people want to hug and kiss and be with each other all of the time."

Victor knew he wanted to be with Dennis all the time before he left, but he had never thought of kissing him or hugging him—although, in that moment, the thought was not particularly distasteful. He hugged and kissed his mother and father all the time. He thought he wanted to kiss Mrs. Terhart, and he knew he would like to hug her. But he didn't say this. Instead he said, "Something is happening in me." And then, "I'm scared."

And Mrs. Terhart—not Victor this time—began to cry.

Justine was driving too fast. She was helping to arrange a new clothing display at the department store, and she had forgotten that it was her turn to pick up Victor. She was not especially worried about him—he was a boy that could handle himself. She would only be twenty minutes late or so, and in that time, what could happen? She looked in the rearview mirror, and her heart skipped a beat or two. Someone was in the back seat! And then she remembered the nature of her cargo: display mannequins. She had forgotten to pull them out and was suddenly mortified to be taxiing these dead things around. They were fully dressed and ready to go, sitting in the backseat of the minivan. She had been moving them across town from one store to another that had found itself suddenly short two or three mannequins. She hated these things. Only vaguely female, they were stark-white, flat-chested, and unrealistically skinny, and they had no facial features to speak of. She knew, in theory, that the idea was that the mannequin was not to detract attention from the clothing, from the product. They needed to be as generic and as invisible as possible while still providing a reasonable facsimile of the human female body from which clothing would realistically hang. Justine knew that she had never purchased a piece of clothing because she had seen it realistically hanging from one of these things. But then again, Justine was not typical of the target demographic. She had exhausted the social security checks from the first part of her life and had to "come out of retirement," as they say—not to earn a living again (her husband made plenty of money), but as a hedge against boredom.

"Climb inside the family wagon, Victor."

Victor got into the van, and he was excited. "Mom, are you building a monster?"

She laughed. "No, sweat pea. I have one already."

"I don't like them," he added, frowning at the passengers in the back seat. "Can we drop them off somewhere?"

"How was your day, Victor? Tell me what you learned."

"I learned three really important things."

"Fire away."

"I like girls."

"Okay."

"Boys are stupid. And a faggot is a bundle of sticks."

Time passed, as it will do. As he watched, Victor started counting recess days. There were thirty days in the rest of the second grade as he collected data for his study of the behaviors of boys and girls. There were 120 days in the third grade, over which he discovered that not only did he seem to like girls better than boys, but they also seemed to take an interest in him. That is, during recess, he was either reading a book or writing in his journal, and despite the bookish behavior that Victor had already discovered was decidedly uncool with his classmates, he noticed things like this: Girl walks by with incredible velocity and says hello, is gone before he can respond. Two girls sneak up behind his bench and try to read what he's writing over his shoulder. Girl stands really close to him in lunch line, touches his hand accidentally three times, and giggles. Receives a greater number of valentines on this holiday than any other boy in the third grade. Overhears two girls talking about how cute he is, despite the reading and the writing. And finally, on one very important occasion, girl named Michelle sticks up for him to Jimmy the gasoline boy, calls Jimmy an asshole, and tells him to stop the name-calling. But all through these 120 days, not once had he been insulted, pushed down, or sawdusted by any girls. It was a strange state of affairs, Victor concluded, as he continued to count the days, mostly uneventful.

On the 140th day of third grade recess, Jimmy the gasoline boy, who happened to be smitten with Michelle (and Victor knew this by observing how mean he was to her), was in rare form. Michelle, braver than any other girl had been so far, was actually speaking to Victor as he sat on the bench in the corner of the field. She had been asking him about what he was reading and writing. Victor, after a year and a half of silence on the subject of monsters to anyone but Dennis and his family, started to tell her that he was writing about his great-granddad.

"Frankenstein?" she asked.

"No," said Victor. "My great-granddaddy didn't have a name."

"That's sad," she said.

"Well, finally, his children named him Adam."

"That was nice of them," she said. Jimmy was standing right behind her, looming.

Jimmy said, "Is Frankenfaggot bothering you?"

"Does it look like he's bothering me, ugly?" And she walked away disgusted.

Jimmy stood there in front of Victor staring him down and Victor just continued looking through his notebook and pretending Jimmy was not there. Finally, upset by the underwhelming impact he was having, he offered up a threat. "Stay away from her, Frankenfucker, or else."

Victor took a deep breath and tried to calm himself. The gasoline smell was stronger than usual, and it made his heartbeat fast in his chest. Was he bathing in the stuff? He looked up at him. Jimmy's hair was a tangle of rats and snags, and Victor thought he could see little pieces of twigs and chunks of dried up dirt curled up inside. *Something might be living in there*, Victor thought. There was a smudge of motor oil on Jimmy's left cheek. Victor said, "She came to *me*. What, you want I should run away from her? And besides, I think she's a nice girl."

"Do you want me to kick your ass?"

Victor thought about how to respond—which amused him, because there was really only one answer. And then he thought that a little humor might relax the tension and bring Jimmy down a bit. He pretended to think about it carefully. "No," he said. "I do not want you to kick my ass."

"Well, I might have to anyway."

By this time, a small crowd had gathered around Jimmy—and Michelle was watching from a distance.

Jimmy continued. "My daddy says faggots burn in hell."

"Well," Victor said. "I imagine they do. They would also burn nicely in a campfire or in a wood stove. I mean, you have to have kindling for a good blaze." Victor thought he was being absolutely brilliant, but he looked around and no one was laughing. Instead, they looked puzzled, utterly confused.

Jimmy believed he was speaking for everyone. "How come you're so fucked up?"

This particular question made no sense to Victor, and he decided not to dignify Jimmy's stupidity with a response. But he felt something going on inside of him that he had only sensed a hint of before, a bubbling up that he had tried to describe to Mrs. Terhart. Something was stirring. He did not know *how* he knew, but he knew what to do. He needed to get away, and suddenly, he stood up in front of Jimmy and the other boys, excused himself politely, worked his way through this knot of children, and walked across the field deliberately in Michelle's direction.

She was looking at him the whole time, and while he did not look up to see her, he could feel her eyes upon him and knew exactly where she was standing. When he was two feet from her he finally looked up. "Can I call you Shelley?" he said.

"All right."

And then he said, "How well do you read?" Victor already knew the answer. He had been watching her all the way through the third grade, bringing books to school, reading them while other kids were still working in small groups, deciphering words with only five or six letters in them.

"I'm pretty good," she said.

"Maybe we could read something together sometime."

"Okay, maybe, yeah." She was smiling, her eyes wide with surprise, and Victor could feel it without looking. He had no desire to push her down, and he could tell that she was not hiding any sawdust. He was warm, and he smiled and knew that he hadn't been this happy since before he learned that Dennis would leave Arizona. Even though he knew from his studies of third grade lovemaking that what he was experiencing was completely backward, he decided not to fight it.

In the next moment, in the split second after this last thought occurred to him, there was a tremendous pressure at his back. He couldn't breathe, and he found himself flying forward, chest first, head thrown back, arms sprawling. He blacked out for a second and sensed a tremendous pounding in his head and in his chest. When he opened his eyes he saw and smelled grass and dirt. He turned himself around and saw Jimmy the gasoline boy standing above him, several boys around him laughing, and the sun, right behind them, blinding and hot as he lay on the ground. Jimmy had reached down and grabbed Victor by the shirt. Victor saw Jimmy's right arm winding back, his hand in a fist, and then direct sunlight: Jimmy had vanished, as if a monstrous wind had simply blown him away. The boys were laughing now, hysterically, and then the sun was blocked now by another figure. Shelley. Michelle. She had pushed him aside before he could throw the punch, and now Jimmy was also lying on the dirt and the grass. "There's only one boy here going to rot in hell, and it's not Victor. You're a coward, Jimmy." And she held out her hand for Victor. He grabbed it and she pulled him up.

As the two of them walked back toward the school building, Victor could not stop crying. They were convulsive, deep sobs. A stabbing sensation. It would not stop. At first, Shelley was walking along beside him and holding his hand, but then they stopped walking and she was holding him and that made him cry all the more violently. There was no physical pain; he was not hurt, did not have any injuries. It was inconceivable to Victor how Jimmy could hate him so completely, and utterly surprising how he could hate Jimmy in return so absolutely that images kept flashing into his brain of how he could hurt him: choke him, pummel him with a stick, bury him alive in the ground. Finally, it was astounding how at the same time, Shelley, a relative stranger, could care for him this way, display this kind of tenderness, and give him this kind of help. All of it contributed to his sobbing. Victor had reached the depths of his grief and simultaneously discovered a pinnacle of ecstasy he had never imagined.

He lost count of the rest of the days in the third grade.

Of Teachers, Parents, Shelley Reading Shelley, and Paradise Lost and Regained

When Mrs. Terhart transferred from teaching the second to the fourth grade, Victor felt that either God or Mrs. Terhart had done him a personal favor. He briefly entertained a fantasy that Mrs. Terhart was in love with him and couldn't bear any longer to be without him, and he tried one day to get a confession from her. She explained to him that while she was indeed very fond of Victor, she made the move because in general she was partial to bigger, older kids, and that she liked that curriculum better. It was just as well, Victor thought; it would be difficult if not impossible to love two women at once in *that way*.

But there may have been other reasons for Mrs. Terhart's move that were not revealed to Victor at the time. She knew she would get most of the children she had in the second grade back again as fourth graders—and this was a reason even more salient to Mrs. Terhart than the ones she gave to Victor. She wanted to see them grow up, wanted to watch their relationships deepen, wanted to deepen her own connection to these kids and to teach them still the things she had not had an opportunity yet to teach them. Why could she not have told him these things? She had her reasons.

And Victor, on that occasion, was more easily satisfied than he had typically been with minimal explanation of an important problem. He had other things on his mind—he had Michelle very much on his mind.

"Jesus H. Christ," Justine said to her husband. "Isn't it a little bit early for him to be having girls over to the house?"

"It's innocent enough. After all," and he said this with just a hint of sarcasm, "she's helping him learn the lore. They are reading the Mary Shelley, or at least trying to. Pretty damn impressive for fourth graders, if you ask me."

"Do you think it's a little odd, his nicknaming her that?"

"Nicknaming who what?"

"He's calling her Shelley, this girlfriend of his."

"Maybe that's her name."

"Michelle."

"It's close enough. It'd be a lot different if her real name were Beulah. But at any rate, if it is a little odd, you and your mother have only yourselves to blame."

Victor's dad, Mark, was an accountant who worked hard and made money to provide his family with a standard of living that was, if not extravagant, extremely comfortable, especially as it was supplemented with Justine's income. But he put in long hours, and outside of the running and jumping and hugging he received from Victor when he came home at night and conversations he would try to have at least once before the boy went to bed every evening, he had a very hands-off approach to fathering. Justine filled him in on most of the news regarding his son, and it was almost as if he was hearing about something not quite connected to himself—another man's kid, perhaps. But Victor *was* his kid; he was sure of that. Mark had a similar quiet demeanor and the same sort of quizzical approach to things he was interested in, and he could see his facial features and physical tics in the boy. And that pleased him, made him feel like he was witnessing his own childhood—almost an out-of-body experience. Going into the marriage, though, he knew from the moment the question of children surfaced that his son's childhood would be very different from his own. Justine insisted from the very beginning, as did Grandma Elizabeth, that any child of theirs would know the family history.

There was a part of him that resisted all of this Frankenstein history (in his mind, he called it "hooey," but never out loud). He managed to repress this doubt, and sometimes he wondered at his good fortune. Early in his relationship with Justine, he really could not be sure whether or not he had landed himself a bona fide nut for a partner—but as time passed, he would learn that there was hardly one single other characteristic of hers that was at all eccentric or dangerous or worrisome. He really did not believe his wife was 120 years old (it was hard to explain those social security checks, though, and the photos of her and her dead husband, and the other little artifacts—clothing and antique trinkets and such), but he went along with it and the whole monster tale because there seemed to be so many other wonderful attributes to focus on. Overall, his life with Justine had been peaceful and mundane. His relationship with his mother-in-law, however, was a different story.

"Since Mom's coming over tonight, maybe she can help them," Justine said.

"Lord. I wouldn't trust her as a chaperone. She'd probably be giving them pointers all right—and it wouldn't be about reading Shelley."

Mark had always felt that Elizabeth was dangerous in some vague, unexplainable way. Likely, it was because he was afraid that Justine might become more like her. Elizabeth was passionate and worried about nothing—an idealist. Justine was a mostly calm, logical woman given sometimes to thinking too hard about things—a realist. They were opposites, it seemed, in so many ways, but they rarely fought openly, and Justine was, in Mark's view of things, far too tolerant of her mother's idiosyncrasies and wild ideas. What frightened Mark, even though he would not admit it to anyone, was the possibility that if Justine did not openly oppose her mother, she would be influenced by her and come under a spell of some kind, and that all hell would then break loose. He was happy, at least, in his mother-in-law's stance against monster making. But holy St. Francis, he thought, she sure did talk about it enough, on and on and on—so what difference did it make after all what she believed?

When Elizabeth arrived for the monthly family dinner, Justine told her of Victor's plans for the evening, and she was alive with the possibilities.

"So soon? That kid is brilliant! Things are coming along quite nicely," she said.

"Excuse me?" Mark was instantly taken aback. "What *things,* Elizabeth?"

"You are such a prude, Mark. Justine, why did you marry such a prude?"

"Oh, Mom."

Mark could not let that stand. "That's all you have to say? Your mother insults me and you say, 'Oh, Mom.'"

"She's kidding, Mark."

"No, I am not kidding. You will know when I am kidding. I am not kidding now. The both of you sometimes act like you must contain everything and everyone, that you must protect yourselves and others from living! My God, though, I cannot wait to meet this little girl. And to think he calls her Shelley."

"What do you think of that, Mom?" Justine asked, revisiting the question she posed earlier to her husband.

"It's sweet, dear. It's the sweetest thing I have ever heard."

Another thing that bothered Mark about Elizabeth was this off-the-charts kind of excitement she exhibited for all things romantic. Love, it seemed, was at the center of her universe. It came before all else. No matter that it concerned a nine-year-old boy. No matter that, according to her own account, she had been in love more times than a human being has fingers and toes and seemed not to regret a single one of them. No matter that, despite her advanced age, Mark found her terrifyingly sexy. At times, he could not believe that Elizabeth was old enough to be Justine's mother, despite her insistence that she was, what, one hundred and fucking forty-two years old? Sometimes it was just too much.

They had agreed to attempt *Frankenstein* together. It would be an ambitious endeavor, they both understood, without any guarantee of success. But earlier in the school year, when Victor had suggested this to Michelle, the task was met with an almost ecstatic commitment on both sides. It took weeks of planning, mostly in building up the courage to ask their parents' permission. They approached it with some apprehension that they didn't quite understand, as if they were proposing something illicit, or at least something that only much bigger kids would be allowed to do. But permission was granted and arrangements were made. She would bring the best and biggest dictionary she could find in her father's study, he would gather up the notes he had collected in his journal over the last couple of years, and together they would crack the code, they would decipher the story, and they would know for themselves from this primary document the true history of Victor's beginnings. Shelley had been visibly touched (Victor remembered her slight shudder) at not merely the invitation to read this book with him, but also to learn that he had nicknamed her after this most illustrious writer. "My goodness," she had said when he told her the author's name.

After dinner, as he sat in his bedroom cradling the book in his hands, touching its cover, running his fingers over the slightly raised letters of its title, and breathing in the smell of the type on the page, he was thinking about how amazing it was that, while he felt very much in love with this girl, there still had been no injuries inflicted between them. He concluded that this was no ordinary love affair, and that both he and Michelle were no ordinary fourth graders.

All three adults were standing nervously in the kitchen and called out at once when the car pulled up in the driveway. "She's here." There was a brief meet and greet at the front door between the adults in Victor's household and Michelle and her mother. Mark was grateful that Elizabeth behaved herself. He was happy, too, that this very nice woman who came to the door with her daughter seemed to have no inclination what the family believed regarding the subject of this sweet little reading project. And there was an awkward moment when the girl's mother walked away, the door closed behind her, and these three big people just stood there and watched as Victor approached his friend. They were transfixed and silent.

Victor walked slowly toward her as if he was walking down the aisle of a church.

It was too much for Mark. "My gosh, Michelle, what do you have there?"

"*The Oxford English Dictionary*," she said. "Abridged, of course."

"Of course." Mark could hardly keep from laughing.

"Come on," Victor said. "We can go into the library." And they were off into the room in which Justine and Mark kept all of the books passed down from the preceding generations of both sides of the family. There were more books gathered there than Michelle had ever seen in anyone's home. She was stunned and spent the first few minutes just walking around the shelves and looking. "Some of these books look old."

"They are very old," said Victor, and he heard his grandmother call out from the other room.

"Call me if you need me, kids."

And he heard his father say, "They'll be just fine, Elizabeth."

Settling down in the two chairs around at a reading table that Victor's father had built just for him, an antique mission lamp illuminating the sacred thing spread out before them both, the first difficulty they experienced came to them on the title page. Michelle read out loud, "*Frankenstein, or the Modern Prometheus.* Hey, Victor, what's a Prometheus?" And before he could even answer that he did not know, she was digging through the Oxford. "It says here that Prometheus is a Greek god, a Titan who stole fire from heaven for mankind, and as a punishment, he was chained to a rock, where, daily, an eagle devoured his liver, which was made whole again at night."

"Wow," said Victor.

"Poor Prometheus," said Michelle.

"What's a liver?"

"Oh, it's an organ. It's in here somewhere," Michelle said, her hands moving over her midsection. "I don't think you can live without one."

"That's why they replaced it every day, so that he'd keep living."

"Not very nice of them, though, if that eagle was just gonna keep coming back."

"Have you ever had liver for dinner?" Victor had horrible associations with a family dinner several months back made doubly horrible by tons of fried onions. "It's not good," he said.

"Should we read the author's introduction?" Michelle asked, and Victor could tell she was very much interested in hearing what her namesake had to say about the book they were about to read. He agreed unreservedly.

Michelle continued to read out loud, and beyond being fascinated by the words she was reading, Victor was also surprised at how taken he was with her voice, steady and quiet, but expressive. Victor thought it was the most beautiful sound he had ever heard. She stumbled a bit over long sentences and words like "intrusion" or "distinguished" or "succession," but the more she read, the better she read, and before long it seemed like she didn't even have to pause.

They understood that the introduction was Mary Shelley's story about how the story of *Frankenstein* came into being. She was writing it at the request of her publishers for a new edition, many years after the book was first published. She talked about how, as a child, despite having literary parents, she preferred dreaming to writing because she thought her writing was too imitative, while her dreaming to her was wholly original and private. Skipping over her childhood in about a paragraph, she continued to speak about how her husband encouraged her to write, to "enroll myself on the page of fame," something that was important to her then, but to which in time she would become "infinitely indifferent." She talked about how she and her husband spent the summer in Switzerland with a poet named Lord Byron who was writing a poem that Mary found very impressive, a poem that "seemed to stamp as divine the glories of heaven and earth." Victor and Michelle both had troubles with this phrase, although they liked the way it sounded. It took them maybe fifteen minutes to figure out that the word "stamp" in this context was a fancy way of saying "make," that the poem Byron was writing *made* everything under the sun seem divine. But wasn't heaven *above* the sun? Michelle suggested that maybe the word "heaven" referred not to the literal heaven, but to the sky, in which case it would be *under* the sun.

The weather in Switzerland was bad. They entertained themselves by reading ghost stories. And then Lord Byron suggested that they all write their own. Mary's husband could not be bothered with a "story," so he wrote a poem instead. There was a man with them named Polidori who wrote a story that was in Mary's opinion "very shocking and wrong of course," and Lord Byron cheated by adding on to something he had already been drafting.

Next in her introduction, Mary Shelley spoke of her desire to rival the efforts of her friends and husband. She wanted to inspire horror, dread, and blood curdling and to "quicken the beatings of the heart," and if she could not do those things, the task would not be worth the effort. It took her a long time to think of something good, and her friends and husband started to give her a hard time. And then there came a paragraph that Victor and Michelle could make neither head nor tail of, something about Hindu elephants supporting the world while standing on turtles, another something about invention out of chaos, and still some other strange thing about Columbus and an egg.

And then Mary spoke of listening to her husband and Lord Byron wax philosophic about the principles of life and about this guy Darwin, who supposedly made a worm he'd been storing for a while move on its own inside a glass case. From there, the talk turned to the possibilities of bringing various body parts together, manufacturing a creature, and of reanimating the dead!

This was a revelation to Victor, and Michelle was not a little bit surprised herself. What they understood was that the idea of making monsters was inspired by this overheard conversation and was not original to Mary, nor was it considered by her to be a story of ostensibly true events. It was like this, according to Mary Shelley: Having heard this talk between her husband and Lord Byron, she couldn't sleep. As she tossed and turned, into her mind came the vision of this "pale student of unhallowed arts kneeling beside the thing he had put together." She had found her ghost story. She began to write and was encouraged by her husband to keep going, to make it longer, and eventually, it was finished.

All that was left for Michelle and Victor to discover from the introduction was that Mary Shelley outlived her husband and that the story she wrote she credited to their continuing conversations before he died. She concluded by saying that, as far as revision is concerned, the story had changed very little from its original form.

There was silence in the library.

"She made it up, Victor," Michelle said. "It's not a true story."

"That can't be," Victor said, and he looked at his friend, looked directly into her eyes. Her eyes were beginning to water a bit. And even though a momentary flood of fear pulsed through his powerful little fourth grade brain, Victor could tell that the look she was giving him was one of sympathy and not of derision. But all the faith in the family stories and in Grandma Elizabeth, whom he loved more than anything in the world, was suddenly on shaky ground, and all that he could think to do was to say one more time, "That can't be."

Then there was a voice from the library doorway. "Can I come in, kids?"

"Grandma, she made it up," Victor said, whirling around in his chair to greet her. "She made it up!"

"Hold on, Victor. Slow down. Tell me what you understand."

And as Grandma Elizabeth floated into the room and sat down beside the two children in Mark's reading chair, Victor gave the rundown of the childhood dreaming, the weekend in Switzerland, the ghost story contest, the overheard conversation, and then the writing of the story. "Okay, that all sounds about right," Grandma said with a calm that baffled Victor and Michelle. "There are two things you must know," she continued. "First, do you know why she wrote this introduction?"

Michelle, ever the dutiful student, was first with the answer. "Her publishers asked her to write it."

"Yes. Exactly. Good. Now, let me ask you this, kids. Why couldn't they leave the story to stand on its own? Why do we need this introduction?"

"So that people would know why she wrote the story," said Victor.

"And why do they need to know that, pray tell?"

It was Michelle's turn. "Because it's interesting?"

"Maybe."

"Then why, Grandma?" Victor was tired of questions. He wanted answers.

"You will learn more about this when you get older," she said and then gave them a little history lesson. In the nineteenth century, and especially coming from a woman, the Frankenstein story was too shocking, too depraved, and too strange for public consumption. It caused quite a disturbance. People were frightened; their worlds were shaken. And there was something else to consider: her publishers, in part in an effort to protect Mary's reputation, but mostly to sell more books, asked her thirteen years later to write this new introduction, hoping it would soften the impact a little, hoping it would explain to a superstitious and fearful public how it came to pass that a woman, a perfectly sane and moral woman, could write such a story. And Mary was no fool, Elizabeth told them. Despite the work and influence of her mother, a very famous activist for women's rights, Mary knew that without this explanation, her book might have never reached a more popular audience.

"So," Victor said and paused. There was another difficult question to ask. "So she made all of *this* stuff up? She lied about all of *this*?"

"Victor, not exactly, dear. I believe every word of this introduction: the dreaming, Switzerland, ghost stories, overheard conversations, the encouragement of a husband—all of it is true. But there are some things she does not say outright. And here's the second thing you need to know." In her grandmotherly way, Elizabeth taught Victor and Michelle about *referencing the text* as she read out loud the following passage: "My imagination, unbidden, possessed and guided me, gifting the successive images that arose in my mind with a vividness far beyond the usual bounds of reverie."

"What does it mean, Grandma Elizabeth?" But even as he asked the question, he had an intuitive sense about an answer, could feel almost within his bones an affinity for this *unbidden imagination,* for feeling possessed or visited, guided and gifted.

Grandma Elizabeth did not need to answer, and she kept still and silent. The two children looked at her, in awe of the idea before them, an idea almost too large for their young minds to hold on to. But they persisted and held on, and for a moment with Grandma Elizabeth, they resonated together an understanding of this undeniable truth: Mary Shelley was no prophetess, no divinely inspired scribe chosen by the hand of God to tell this story. What Mary Shelley characterized as a profound moment of spontaneous inspiration was more likely a visitation, in spirit, flesh, or some other mode of communication, on this evening or years before in the young woman's childhood from the only person alive who actually knew the story young Mary needed to tell.

Of Paradise Lost, Again

Victor and Michelle agreed to meet twice a week to work their way through Victor's family history, Mary Shelley's *Frankenstein*. After the problem of the story's authenticity was solved, a new problem cropped up that Grandma Elizabeth also helped them work through. Apparently, the only real artifice on Shelley's part, as opposed to confessing the true nature of the inspiration, was to create, instead of a typical nineteenth-century omniscient narrator, a character, if you will, a Mr. Robert Walton, who would report the story of Dr. Frankenstein through letters to his beloved sister Margaret. One of the certainties that became clear to these children right away was that they were in the hands of a very clever writer indeed. Their awe of her grew with every turn of the page.

It was an early spring evening in Arizona, warm and clear, when the two children, sitting in the family library, traveled to the wintry North Pole with Robert Walton, a scientist, an explorer hoping to clear passage for future sailors. Not entirely altruistic, Walton is driven by a passion to explore and discover, The vocation was expressly forbidden to him by a father who was also in the exploration business, but who was, fortunately for Robert Walton, at the time of his own voyage, deceased.

In his letters to his sister Margaret, two things caught Victor's attention and made him think he was in the presence of a kindred spirit—in this author, this character, or this friend who continued to read out loud so beautifully and musically. Michelle read of Walton's correspondence, "You may deem me romantic, my dear sister, but I bitterly feel the want of a friend." And then later in the same letter, "There is something at work in my soul which I do not understand." Were the two ideas connected? Victor couldn't be sure. He just knew that both of these statements resonated with him in a way that he could not articulate. And when Robert Walton finally found his friend in this stranger found floating on an icecap, utterly on the verge of death by exposure and exhaustion, when he takes him in, nurses him back to health, and shares with him the idea that a person could never be truly happy without friendship, Victor found another kindred spirit in the voice of the stranger. "I once had a friend, the most noble of human creatures, and am entitled, therefore, to judge respecting friendship. You have hope, and the world before you, and have no cause for despair. But I—I have lost everything, and cannot begin life anew."

Victor knew already, or thought he knew from the family stories, that the stranger, Dr. Victor Frankenstein himself, was referring to the loss of his best friend, Henry, and it reminded Victor now of his own lost friend. It seemed to Victor that after the loss of Dennis, life had in fact began anew with his discovery of Michelle—but he began to think about that first friendship again and to suddenly shudder with an unaccountable fear that Michelle was already drifting away from him.

"Shelley?"

"Yeah."

"Do you love your girlfriends?"

"What do you mean?"

"Do you think about them when they're not with you?"

"Yes."

"If your best friend right now moved away from you, or died, how would you feel?"

"Terrible."

"Because you love her?"

"Yes."

"I loved my friend Dennis, and those kids call me a faggot. I love Mrs. Terhart, and then I'm a butt-kisser. I love my mother, and I'm a mama's boy. It seems like people don't want you to love people."

Michelle was thinking it's because they don't love. They aren't loved. They don't know how and nobody ever told them. But she said to Victor, "Maybe, yeah."

"I would die if I couldn't love people."

"It's like our stranger, here, on Walton's ship," Michelle said. "He seems to be dying without his friends. Just like that."

"And his monster."

"Hmm?"

"You'll see." There seemed to be something in the room with them that needed space, so they were silent together for quite some time before Victor spoke again. "Shelley?"

"Yeah."

He squirmed in his chair, fiddled with the novel's pages. He changed his mind. "Forget it."

"Okay," she said and began reading out loud at chapter one, in the doctor's own words as he began to tell Robert Walton his lamentable tale, beginning with his own family's history and makeup.

Victor and Michelle read of the great charitable nature of Dr. Frankenstein's father: how, in trying to help a friend fallen on difficult times, he searches for him and finds the friend on his deathbed in the arms of his daughter, now destitute and penniless without him; how Frankenstein's father would take this woman, Caroline, as his wife, love and worship her, have a child with her, the first Victor Frankenstein, and raise this child with "inexhaustible stores of affection from a very mine of love"; how Caroline, like her husband, less the result of his beneficent influence and more owing to what her own experience had taught her about charity and mercy, took great joy in helping the underprivileged; how Caroline, with Victor in tow, would find Elizabeth the First as an orphan with a family more abjectly impoverished than it would be possible to imagine and offer to adopt the child. Thus, Victor and Michelle learned of the original family: a loving mother and father, a young boy blessed with the gifts of a charmed childhood, and an adopted daughter, an angel in corporeal form, who would become the boy's best friend—or, in the words of Dr. Frankenstein, "my more than sister—the beautiful and adored companion of all my occupations and my pleasures."

The two fourth graders paused and listened once again to the silence at the end of chapter one.

Finding herself inexplicably gleeful, Michelle said, "Boy, it all sounds so wonderful. They were all such good people. And they all loved each other so much." And then she was sad, because she knew the direction things would eventually go. "What went wrong, Victor? Do you know?"

"I know a little, but I don't want to ruin it." He didn't say this, but he also didn't want to be wrong in the event that what was revealed in this book somehow didn't match up with what he had heard or thought he remembered. One thing was certain, Victor thought, as he reflected on the very first description of his grandmother's namesake: Grandma Elizabeth, for some crazy reason (crazy because even Victor knew it was physically impossible) seemed a complete embodiment of this little girl in chapter one, only older, a lot older, and considerably more modern.

There was an adult voice, Mark's, at the door, saying how late it was for a school night, that Michelle should probably call her mom, and that there were some cookies in the kitchen before she had to go. And so Victor and Michelle closed the book for another few days, had themselves some chocolate chip cookies and milk, and said good-bye to each other at the door, brimming with anticipation for their next encounter.

Absences from work scattered throughout the year, and the entire previous week lost, Mrs. Terhart sat behind her desk and breathed deeply in and out. There was some pain, though, today. It was harder to relax. She looked around at the finger paintings and cutouts and construction paper models, at the posters of animals and countries of the world, and then she closed her eyes and saw nothing but sparks in the dark behind her eyelids. Then nothing at all. She was tired. It was hard to stay awake. She opened her eyes again, looked over at the chalkboard at her sentence models, looked at the poster she had created herself, titled "An Invitation to Read," a list of all the best reasons to do so. This, she thought, was a sacred place. It had been so long since she had been inside of a church, but she felt often in her classroom the way she had felt as a child sitting in awe at the wonderful mysteries of faith and the magnificent miracles of Jesus. She knew all along this was something like that. It was work that required the same kind of faith, a job at which you could witness daily the miracle of learning and the tremendous power of the brain, the phenomenal gifts of the human spirit made manifest in these children's lives. This was a sacred place.

She managed to get through the first few hours without a hitch, but then she became increasingly weak and tired. The kids were happy to have her back, and for a while, their energy bolstered her spirits. But when they left for recess, she stayed behind, alone in her classroom, exhausted, unable to move herself to the lunchroom. She blamed the way she felt right then on the weight of what she knew she had to do when the kids came back in from recess. It was a heavy lesson indeed.

The principal and a counselor were in the room on that afternoon in April of the fourth grade year when Mrs. Terhart started talking. "Children. I need your best attention right now. It must be quiet in here so that you can hear what I'm saying. Johnny, please. Eyes up front, people. Teresa, not now, hon. Do you see the signal, everyone? And what does it mean? Okay. Quiet now. Good. Thank you. Most of you have noticed that I have been absent a lot lately. We have had several substitutes, haven't we? I want to explain something to you that will help you understand why I have been gone so much lately. I have been gone because I am very ill. I have a sickness. It's called pancreatic cancer. I am going to the doctor for some medicine, but the medicine makes me very sick, too. That means that I will be gone more often now. I will be too sick to be with you, not because what I have is contagious—you will not get this from me—but because I will be too weak to do a good job for you. I want you to know how much I care about all of you. I love you all very much, and I will miss you. But I have to do what is best for me now, and we will have to trust that your substitutes will do their very best. And I want you to promise me that you will do your best for them. Can I get that commitment from everyone? That's how you can best help me, by doing for your substitute teachers exactly what you would do for me. Okay? Does anybody have any questions?"

Most of the children were crying because they understood without being told. A few of them, though, were not yet sure exactly what all of this meant, and there was one kid who was brave enough to ask, "Are you going to die?"

There was silence for a long, long time as Mrs. Terhart looked inside herself for the courage she would need to say the words to all of these children.

And then Victor stood up from his desk and looked at her with tears streaming down his face and a terrible pain making itself known to his classmates. "No! She will become light," he said. And he said it over and over as he ran from the room, into the hallway, and finally out of the school building, where he ran and ran and ran.

He knew his way home well enough, even though he had never traversed this distance on foot. He knew it would take him a long time, but it was time that he needed, away from people, away from other children, away from this horrible news. She would become light, he kept saying. After awhile it ceased to be a comfort—or rather, he understood that it had never been a comfort, knowing that he would much rather have a flesh and blood Mrs. Terhart than a ghostlike one. And then he was embarrassed for having said it, for having stood up in front of all of those kids, for having been crushed so easily, and for diverting attention to himself that rightfully belonged to his dying fourth grade teacher. "I'm sorry, Mrs. Terhart. I'm sorry," he kept saying. And what in God's name was pancreatic cancer? He would look it up when he got home, and he would learn about it. And he walked and walked. At one point, he knew which direction to go but was unsure of the street to take. He took the first of two that were situated close together and appeared to be moving in parallel lines. He would learn about pancreatic cancer, and he would find out how to make Mrs. Terhart better again.

The phone call home came almost immediately after Victor left the school. Justine called Mark at his office, and then, against his wishes, she called her mother. Elizabeth was there within twenty minutes. Still no Victor. Mark left work and drove straight to the school, and from there, he tried to find his son. He drove around the neighborhood down any street that could eventually lead Victor home, and when he realized that Victor might be lost, he started driving the streets that would never get Victor home. Still no Victor. Justine had called the police, so Mark knew he was not the only one looking. Sooner or later, they would find him.

Victor walked, oblivious to his surroundings. He felt he was moving in the right direction. That was all. Mostly, he struggled to keep himself from moaning or howling at the sky. He was choking on sobs.

"Look who's here."

A voice he recognized brought a double sense of doom into his heart. He thought he could smell him all the way from the street; it was as if the sound of the voice and the smell of the kid were one and the same, or that one could invoke the other. Victor had two questions: what was Jimmy doing out of school, and, of all roads, why did he come down this road?

"Skipping out early, huh, Frankenboy?"

Victor's heart was pounding and he kept his feet moving.

"Hey, Victor, don't be afraid. Come here, dimwit. I won't hurt you."

Something made him stop. Victor stopped walking and turned to face him.

There were two other boys with him just outside of Jimmy's garage. There were a half a dozen cars in varying degrees of disrepair, not half of them operable or road-worthy, scattered in front of the garage in the driveway and parked along the street. The three boys bobbed in and out between cars and greeted Victor at the end of the driveway.

"You been crying? Somebody beat you up again?" The two other boys laughed. "I tell you, what, Victor," Jimmy said. "You're skipping school, for one, and that makes you a little bit more okay in my book. But I still think you might be a fag. I'll give you one more chance to prove you're not a fag. Do you smoke?"

"Uh, no, I don't."

"Well, we'll have to change that, won't we? Fags don't smoke. You gotta smoke if you're not a fag. Light one up for him, Doofus." Doofus, apparently, was one of the other boys. The one who answered pulled out a box of matches from his pants pocket, and from the inside of his coat, he pulled out a package of cigarettes. Doofus, a fat boy, and ugly, put the cigarette in his mouth, lit a match, held the match to the end of the cigarette, and inhaled, and when he did that, the end of the cigarette turned a bright orange. He handed the lit cigarette to Victor.

Jimmy said, "Now, you take a big drag off of this thing, and I promise I won't ever bother you again."

Things were about as bad as they could get, Victor thought, so why not indulge for a moment in an activity that might relieve at least some of the bother? If he didn't have to put up with Jimmy's harassment almost every day at school, he and Shelley could work harder on *Frankenstein*, and then maybe, too, he might be able to concentrate more effectively on creating a new pancreas for Mrs. Terhart. Whatever may come of it, Victor was following some inner guidance that told him that right now, the thing to do would be to take a drag off of this stupid little stick of brown leafy stuff wrapped in thin white paper. What could it hurt?

He inhaled. Immediately, he began coughing, a hacking cough, a gagging cough, and there was a burning, a terrible burning inside his throat and chest. His convulsions caused him to lose complete control of his limbs and appendages. As the boys were laughing, the cigarette in between his thumb and forefinger was let loose somehow, and the burning cinder flew toward Jimmy. He caught the thing in his hand, and in a moment there was fire. Jimmy's hands and then his little boy garage outfit were in flames. Victor, still coughing, remembered stop, drop, and roll, and though hacking and gagging, he was able somehow to call out in clear, decisive tones. "Run, Jimmy, run!" And as Jimmy ran, he burned.

In all of the chaos of search and worry, worry and search, they had failed to look to see if he was home. He must have gone straight out back through the fence and likely, from the looks of it, he had been home for the better part of a half an hour. Justine called Mark on his cell phone and called the police.

Victor was out digging in the yard. A foot or two down into the dirt he found a stone that fit into the palm of his hand. He covered it with damp dirt. He used water from the birdbath to make mud. He covered the dirty stone with mud. He picked handfuls of grass and then pressed the grass into the mud on the stone. It was exactly how he imagined it. He was determined to finish this project.

Elizabeth had approached him quietly from behind.

"Hey there, Victor. What are you doing?"

"I'm building a pancreas."

"No, Victor, that's not how it's done."

"Then when she dies you must bring her back."

"No, Victor, I can't do that. The art is dead. No one knows how. And it's best that way."

"How can it be best?"

"Trust me."

"Then help me make this. Help me make a pancreas for Mrs. Terhart. Help me save her life."

And Elizabeth sat down in the dirt with him and held the boy in her arms. He wrapped his arms around her waist, put his head into her lap, and sobbed—for the boy that he thought he killed, and for the teacher he would lose.

"Some good will come of this," she said.

Of Anger, Fear, and Recess

Jimmy survived but suffered severe burns on his hands, on both of his arms, and across his torso. Victor's role in the event would be obscured, omitted by all three of the witnesses because they each feared that their own part in the accident would come to light. Before the accident, Jimmy's father had beaten him multiple times for playing with matches, for playing in the garage, for playing with matches inside the garage, and for the oddest and most disconcerting of Jimmy's behaviors: rubbing gasoline into his hands. And Jimmy remembered the threat, all too vividly, that if his father ever caught him smoking anywhere near the house, he'd murder him. He used those words. "I will murder you, so help me God, if I ever catch you smoking around this house. Do you hear me?" Jimmy had heard, loud and clear, but he would discover, soon enough and repeatedly, how difficult it was sometimes, when what you know is best and what you want to do are in conflict, to choose the one over the other. And there was this other difficulty, too, in following through with his father's wishes: a lit cigarette often dangled from his father's lips as he threatened him against smoking, and a cuff across the face often accompanied the lectures against harassing other kids, especially ones that were smaller and weaker than Jimmy. "Pick on kids your own damn size, shrimpbait." And so Jimmy and his two accomplices lied about how the accident occurred, saying that the fire had started as they were killing ants with a magnifying glass and had accidentally caught fire to some leaves in the dirt, which spread to Jimmy's gasoline-soaked hands and clothes as he tried to snuff out the flames. It wasn't a bad lie, as lies go; it came from their own handy real-life experience with a magnifying glass of a few days back when something like this almost actually occurred.

Doofus, apparently, had the forethought to hide the incriminating evidence. While his friend ran around in a blaze, he carefully picked up the burnt matches and the mostly unsmoked cigarette from off the concrete of the driveway. The other boy had started running from the moment he saw fire and never looked back. Jimmy, in his own way, had seen nothing remiss in the behavior of his two friends. Each of them did exactly as he would have done in the same situation. But Victor, on the other hand …

Jimmy was preoccupied with Victor for weeks afterwards. Not only did Jimmy hold Victor responsible for the burns, but worse, he felt humiliated and stupid for falling for such a lame trick. He knew what to do in case of fire, but the panic had made him susceptible to suggestion—and the way Victor yelled "Run, Jimmy, run" with such certainty and authority kept him moving despite the other voice in his head imploring the opposite instruction: Stop. Drop. Roll. Maybe the voice wasn't in his head after all. He had a vague recollection of his father out there in the street, yelling something at the top of his lungs after all three boys had disappeared from the scene. Nevertheless, he knew Victor had acted in a way that exacerbated his injuries and could have killed him, had Jimmy not heeded the voice inside his head or coming from his dad, whichever it was. Somehow, at some point in time, Jimmy knew this: Victor would pay.

And Victor, for his part, said nothing to anyone about the cigarette incident and tried as best he could to forget about it, to pretend it was a dream—because, he thought, if he were discovered as the perpetrator of this crime, he would go to jail, and he would not be able to continue the two most important activities of his life: reading *Frankenstein* with Michelle and finding a cure for pancreatic cancer.

Days later, as Victor rode the bus to school, he was still thinking about Jimmy's burning. He was, of course, relieved to learn that Jimmy had not been killed—or as relieved as could be expected on learning that such a person would still wander the earth. At least it set his mind at ease about going to jail. But somehow, this was not altogether a comfort. He believed that now he would be in greater danger than ever from this tyrant who was capable of who knew what. Victor considered turning himself in as a way of obtaining some protection. Would they still put him in jail even if he had not been successful in killing his victim? He thought they would. He had heard or read somewhere about people in jail for "attempted murder." And then the question would come: Had he intended to kill that boy? What had he been thinking? Nothing. It had just happened. He tried to erase the record of the fantasies he had entertained about Jimmy—the pummeling, the beating with a stick, the burying—but it was of no use. "I have thought these things," Victor said out loud, and a kid sitting in front of him on the bus turned around and glared.

There was another possibility that came to him as he reflected on his sociological findings of the third grade: Jimmy, having been harmed in this most hideous way, had taken it as a sign of affection and had now decided to become Victor's friend. He could not convince himself of this, despite all of the evidence he had collected to the contrary, and so he returned in very short order to being afraid for his life.

He wished Michelle were with him, that she lived along this bus route. What a phenomenal girl she was—so smart, so strong-minded, so sensitive, so full of something Victor wished he could bottle up and carry around with him. Lately, thinking about her, he felt funny inside, like things were spinning in him. Only two other individuals had ever inspired this kind of reaction. One of them was Dennis. The other was that FBI agent from the *X-Files*. Thinking further, however, he had felt something similar in the presence of Mrs. Terhart. Oh, and Grandma Elizabeth. It was always around a beautiful woman, he concluded, with the exception of Dennis, who, while not a woman, was in many ways still quite beautiful. And it wasn't just about the way these people looked. It was almost like a sound he heard when he was around them, like the meditation bell Mrs. Terhart would ring sometimes to get their attention and to make them quiet. It was a sound that penetrated deeply, a sound that deserved his undivided attention and his most reverential quiet.

Sometimes, just being in Michelle's presence made him want to cry.

What would he be crying about? He didn't know, but he was almost certain that it wasn't sadness. He didn't have words to describe to himself or to someone else, verbally or in writing, what he was feeling. Something like gratitude. Something like pure ecstasy. Something that made everything else disappear: all pain, all sorrow, all cruelty, and all death vanished, and it was as though there was never a moment in the history of humankind so pregnant with beauty and goodness. And then there was the knowledge, buried deep down inside somewhere, that it wouldn't last. It made him cry. He couldn't wait to see her again, and he was weeping now on the bus. He got another glare from the kid sitting in front of him. But Victor wasn't ashamed and did not try to hide. The kid shook his head in disbelief, and Victor, tears streaming down his cheeks, smiled at him.

Arriving in the parking lot, getting off the bus, sensing the return of a vague foreboding, he looked around quickly on either side of him as he made his way inside the school. Jimmy would not be back for a while as he recovered from his injuries, and he was very likely laid up in bed or otherwise immobile. But Victor had the strangest feeling, despite the unlikelihood of immediate danger from this horrible kid, that as he entered the school, from some indefinable vantage point, he was being watched.

Mrs. Terhart was in school on that day, bringing such joy into Victor's heart so as to render him completely forgetful of his current danger. And something about Mrs. Terhart's presence in the room made him glow all the more intensely when he was with Michelle. So on that day, he was happy beyond his wildest reckoning. Everything was imbued with goodness. Even math, it seemed, took on a kind of playful sheen, and a vibrancy surged through his entire body as he unraveled the correct solution to a particularly tricky long division problem. And then, remarkably, he found himself thoroughly engaged by a story problem exercise. Jamey wants a new bicycle that costs eighty-nine dollars, and she has fourteen dollars saved up inside her piggy bank. She gets an allowance of five dollars a week from her parents and can earn up to three dollars and fifty cents on a hot afternoon at her own lemonade stand. Victor entertained himself by adding to the problem's complexity in his imagination. How many hot afternoons might there be in your average Arizona April or May? What if her parents gave her a raise for doing an especially thorough job with her chores? She could buy three bikes at that cost in a month's time! What would happen if Jamey decided on a nicer bike? Who was this Jamey girl, anyway, and what was it about that particular bike that appealed to her? Michelle, though she laughed as he worked his way out loud through all of the possibilities in the desk next to her, finally grew impatient and encouraged him to finish the problem so that they could get a head start on their quiet reading time.

During recess, Michelle and Victor walked and talked. In Jimmy's absence, they moved freely and unimpeded through the playground, along the blacktop where the hopscotch, tetherball, four square, and jump rope festivities reigned, and along the grassy field beyond the overgrown baseball diamond where kids chased each other or played on the swing sets and jungle gyms. None of the kids who were Jimmy's friends seemed to show any interest in bothering Victor and Michelle today. In fact, the kids that usually traveled in Jimmy's wake, on all the days that followed the accident during Jimmy's absence, paid absolutely no attention to Victor and Michelle—not even a look of acknowledgement or a sneer of disapproval or a threatening glare. They needed a lead to follow, perhaps, and wanting that, the desire to harass evaporated into thin air. Doofus and the other kid were nowhere to be seen. Victor had not recognized them from school, so they must have gone to another school, been junior high kids, or been just habitually, chronically truant. Victor knew that he had never heard Doofus's name on a role sheet. But despite the relative calm and safety of the day, Victor found himself distracted every now and again by that creepy feeling he had earlier: he was being watched.

Michelle was carrying her copy of *Frankenstein* with her, and they talked about chapter two, having started it the week before at Victor's house and then having finished it on that day during silent reading while most of the other kids were tackling Hardy Boy mysteries, Harry Potter, and picture books or pretending to read Tolkien.

"I think I am a lot like Dr. Frankenstein," Victor said.

"You haven't made any monsters yet."

"No, and I won't, because Grandma says it's wrong."

"So how are you like him, then?"

"I like ideas. I want to know the answers to things. I want to know why things happen. 'The secrets of heaven and earth.' Is there somebody looking at us?"

"Where?"

"Anywhere."

"I don't think so."

"And I want to build a pancreas for Mrs. Terhart."

"You can't do that."

"I tried once, but it wouldn't have worked."

"Victor, it will be years and years and years and years before you can learn how to build a pancreas. Your whole life. I know a friend of my dad's who was almost forty years old before he finally became a doctor. That's how long it takes. Forever."

"It didn't take Frankenstein that long, and he lived centuries ago. And it didn't take his monster that long. In fact, he was faster and smarter."

"Yeah, but."

Michelle and Victor were crossed by children chasing a stray four square ball. They waited patiently and resumed walking when the coast was clear. Michelle was quiet.

"Yeah, but what?" Victor said.

"They weren't building pancreases. They were finding things and making them work again. They were—recycling."

"Okay. I see what you're saying. We're not smart enough yet, are we?"

"I don't think we are, Victor."

"I wish Mrs. Terhart wasn't sick."

"Me too."

"She seems better today."

"It won't last. My daddy says that the kind of cancer she has is about the worst kind a person can get. Six months, maybe."

"I'm scared for her."

"Me too."

"Did you see that?"

"What?"

"Geez, I'm just thinking I keep seeing somebody or feeling somebody watching me." Victor was visibly shaking for a moment as a surge of nervousness worked its way through his body.

"I don't see anything, Victor. You mean a kid on the playground somewhere, spying?"

"Maybe."

"You're not worried about Jimmy, are you? He won't be back for a while. And even when he is back, I doubt he'll be causing much trouble. I hear he was totally burned. So don't worry about him. He won't touch you. Who else could be watching you? An adult? Are you in some trouble? Have you been bad? You're acting kind of guilty."

"Shelley?" There was an urge within him to tell her everything, and it bubbled up to the surface several times before he was successful at swallowing it back down. He dreaded what she would think of him if she knew how bad he had really been, that he was an "attempted murderer." He breathed deeply and immediately felt a wave of something else come over him, warm, enlivening. "Shelley," he said again.

"Yeah."

"I love the way you smell."

"Are you crying?"

"No. I just got something in my eye."

"Let me see. I don't see anything. Victor, you're crying."

"No. I'm not."

"Victor, I think you are the sweetest boy I have ever seen or even heard about."

Victor suppressed a giggle and instead, with his lips closed, smiled so widely that his cheeks stung and some tears gathered into the corners of his mouth. Michelle had difficulty looking back at him, aware of some impropriety that she could not name.

Victor wiped his face with his hand and said, "Let's talk about the book."

"Okay."

Neither one of them spoke. Victor counted thirty seconds in his head.

Michelle picked up on an earlier topic. "In what other ways are you like Dr. Frankenstein as a boy?"

"I love people. And I feel the same way about people in my life as he did about the people in his. I see Dennis in this Henry Clerval guy, the doctor's boyhood friend. And I see you and my grandmother in Elizabeth the First. I sometimes put your face on her when I imagine the story. Or I imagine my grandma as a little girl."

"She is named after her."

"Yes. It was a way of saying sorry, I guess, the whole naming thing, and a way of paying tribute."

"Sorry for what? Tribute to what?"

"You'll see."

"I could tell in chapter two that this is where things get bad for Frankenstein—as he's looking back over his life," Michelle said. "I have to remember that he's still speaking to Robert Walton on that ship in the North Pole. It's easy to forget. Actually, it's really strange when you think about it, but it's really Robert Walton speaking to his sister about what Dr. Frankenstein has said to him! Mary Shelley was so good. But I like that part where he tells him about how, after Agrippa's theories are blown out of the water by this scientist during the thunderstorm, he kind of kicks himself for not recognizing his guardian angel who's trying to send him on another path. Let me look this up." She opened the book to a page she had dog-eared. "He says, 'Destiny was too potent, and her immutable laws had decreed my utter and terrible destruction.'"

"What's 'immutable'?"

"Unchanging."

"Oh."

"Victor, something horrible is going to happen."

"I know."

Justine was running late again from work, and Victor found himself sitting in his classroom to wait at the end of the day instead of wandering around or standing in front of the building. Victor was nervous about wandering around or standing anywhere for any length of time by himself, and he felt cocooned and safe here in room seventeen. His teacher was sitting behind her desk, working with some papers or grading tests, he could not be sure, but she was aware of him there this time and was not sleeping. It took him quite awhile, until the last possible minute before his mother arrived, but he finally found the courage he had been looking for to say what he wanted to say.

"Mrs. Terhart. I want you to know how sorry I am about my behavior the other day. It was wrong of me to stand up and shout, and it was wrong of me to leave the room and walk home."

"Victor, sweetie, that's so nice of you to say. I know you meant no harm by that. And I am just happy that you're all right, that you made it home safely."

"I tried to make you a pancreas."

"That's very thoughtful of you."

"It wouldn't have worked."

"That's all right."

"Are you afraid, Mrs. Terhart?"

"Yes. But not all of the time. Sometimes I feel very brave indeed."

"I'm afraid."

"What are you afraid of, sweetie?"

"I don't know."

"See, that's the scariest thing of all. Once you know what you're afraid of, once you name it, its power over you diminishes. It goes away."

"I know what 'diminishes' means."

"Once you say, for instance, 'I am afraid of being alone,' the fear of being alone diminishes."

"I am afraid of being alone."

"Yes. All of us are at some point or another. But a very famous German poet once wrote, 'We *are* solitary. We may delude ourselves and act as though this were not so. That is all. But how much better it is to realize we are so, yes, even to begin by assuming it.' What do you think of that, Victor?"

"It's beautiful," he said and meant it, but he did not understand.

"And somebody else said, I don't know who, that we are born alone and we die alone. And the crazy thing about it, Victor, is that we are not saddened by this. And the thing our German friend was trying to tell us is that once we realize this and accept it, nothing is frightening. Nothing scares us. We are unshakeable. Anything is possible."

"I love you, Mrs. Terhart," he said. And then, abruptly: "My mother's here."

"I love you too, Victor." And even as he was pivoting quickly to walk away, she gently grabbed his arm, pulled him close, and gave him a squeeze. "Have a nice afternoon," she said, and then Victor flew from her, happy and embarrassed.

She had never before told a student, one on one like this, that she loved him, and as Victor disappeared from the room and ambled out to the parking lot to meet his mother, she understood that she had experienced something crucial, something at the pinnacle of her professional experience and in her interactions with children. And in her last days at work, in her last days on earth, she vowed to herself in that moment that she would never allow an opportunity like that to pass her by, that she would not be afraid to demonstrate or to verbalize her love for these children, many of whom, not including Victor, she thought, would find it nowhere else.

As Victor climbed into the front seat of the family wagon, he noticed the visitors.

"Geez, Mom, when are you going to get rid of these dummies?"

"These are not the same dummies, honey."

"They look like the same dummies."

"Ah, that's because all dummies look alike. At least the ones I work with."

"Oh. I see."

"What did you learn today in school?"

"I learned that you don't have to understand a thing in order to like it."

"Good one."

"I was reminded about how smelling something can make a feeling happen."

"Nice."

"And I think you can tell a fake book from a true book by how often you see yourself inside the story."

"Wow. Anything else?"

"Mommy, I don't like these dummies."

"Is Michelle coming over to read tonight?"

"Yes," Victor sang out loud and immediately forgot about dummies and everything else besides, save Michelle's lovely reading voice—and the number of hours between this moment and the one in which he would be sitting next to her again.

Of Love and Science

Victor had started to worry about himself, when, on reflection, he came to the conclusion that he had rarely ever seen boys cry, he had rarely ever seen men cry, and he certainly had never seen his father cry. Deciding there was something unseemly about the activity, he resolved to try to stop crying. It seemed to make people uncomfortable. And that night, before they dug into their reading, Victor had to ask, to get another perspective.

"Do I cry too much?"

"Don't be silly," Michelle said.

"Men don't cry." He felt the need to pursue it a little further.

"That's stupid," Michelle said with a finality that settled the matter once and for all.

Victor's household had come to refer to these meetings between the two children as "*Frankenstein* nights." They knew they were making tremendous progress, and the adults in the house were pleased and proud. They thought that this might be the beginning of one of the purest, most innocent kinds of courtship young people could know: reading together. They had few illusions about this budding so early into something "serious"; they just knew in their hearts that this was far superior to sneaking kisses underneath bleachers and behind bushes. Mark worried, sometimes out loud, that they might be instead sneaking kisses over Mary Shelley in the library. Justine could convince him that this was not likely happening, while Elizabeth would grow almost giddy at the possibility. Mark was tempted to sneak a peak at them from time to time, but he couldn't force himself to do it. What would he do if he did find them lip-locked? He had no idea.

Victor and Michelle were far from locking lips. But during these sessions, Victor could feel very palpably a kind of excitement the likes of which he had never felt and that he could not name. But he did feel that their being together this way was somehow always on the edge of appropriate and was almost naughty. It was intimacy, pure and simple, and it was wonderful and mysterious—innocent, yes, but nevertheless, almost (need we say it?) sexual. If he were older, or an adult, even, he would have said or thought that the veracity, the sheer breadth of Michelle's intelligence was indeed her most attractive feature. And she smelled wonderful. He found himself always taking very deep breaths around her.

"Look at this, Victor! We're not a quarter of the way through, and we've found Shelley's big idea."

"When the doctor talks to Walton about the pursuit of knowledge?"

"Yes! Let me read this: 'Learn from me,' the doctor says, 'if not by my precepts'—"

"What's a precept?"

"It's an idea—be quiet and listen. … 'if not by my precepts, at least by my example, how dangerous is the acquirement of knowledge and how much happier that man who believes his native town to be the world, than he who aspires to become greater than his nature will allow!' My goodness, Victor, this is so huge. And she was right. My older brother is studying science at school, and he talks to me sometimes about the crazy things scientists can do. Our history is full of this stuff. Who do you think invented these bombs that can blow up the world? Einstein, like, the smartest physicist in the universe, and a peacenik, came up with some theories and formulas that made it possible later to build these stupid bombs that killed entire cities of people in Japan and could now destroy the planet if there was ever a nuclear war. And then there's this whole cloning thing."

"Cloning thing?"

"Yeah. Scientists now know how to make a copy of you, Victor."

"Like Dolly the sheep."

"Yes! Think of it. A scientist could make a whole city of Victors. I mean, I like you and all, I like you a lot—"

"You do?"

"But I wouldn't want a whole city of Victors."

"Why not?"

"You wouldn't be you anymore. You yourself couldn't even tell the original you from another you. And all those Victors could be used for terrible purposes, like a slave race or some underclass that would have to do all the crap jobs or the dangerous work. And then, if somebody decided they didn't like Victor—like if, say, Jimmy was president and he hated all cute boys who cry—he could engineer all cuteness and emotion right out of boys, and then we really would have nothing but a pack of zombies running around. I mean, I'm serious. You know about the Holocaust, right? This terrible man named Hitler thought people were only good if they were blonde haired and blue eyed and spoke perfect German. If Hitler's scientists had learned to clone, they could make only the people they liked—and kill everybody else!"

"That sounds terrible."

"Yes, and Shelley is saying it. That's weird, I feel like I'm talking about myself—Mary Shelley is saying that too much knowledge can be a bad thing."

"If it's used to do bad things."

"Yes, but that's the way it happens every time, though."

"Not every time. Grandma says creating new humans from dead people is wrong, but that's how she got here. She's the daughter of two monsters. And if she didn't exist, I wouldn't exist. What if I were a clone and you didn't know about the other Victors and you still liked me and I was still cute? Wouldn't I still be a good thing and not a bad one even though I was a clone?"

"Probably, Victor."

"God, you smell good."

"Stop smelling me."

"Stop smelling, then."
"Shut up and read."

Victor decided after chapters three, four, and five that he was not as much like Victor Frankenstein as he had originally thought. Dr. Frankenstein, it appeared, was what adults would call obsessive-compulsive. He was egocentric. He had addiction issues. He could benefit today from any number of 12-step programs. Victor and Michelle were discovering how he neglected his friends and family. Yea, verily, it must be said, and they said it to each other, he neglected his own health and sanity to build what would become Victor's great-granddaddy. It was hard not to be somewhat grateful for that neglect, as it did, after all, make Victor's existence possible. But at the end of this particular passage, Victor and Michelle found themselves very disappointed in the great doctor, in agreement with his warning about too much knowledge; sad that he did not have his ethical ducks in a row; and ashamed that through it all, even as he was aware of his descent into madness, he could not stop himself. They were especially shocked to read of his repulsion and disgust at his own creation, of his childlike, no, his babyish desire that Great-Granddad (a *thing,* a *wretch,* a *corpse*) would just go away when he closed his eyes, and of his glee (he called it a "great good fortune") when Great-Granddaddy, unable to speak or understand anything about what had happened to him, does in fact wander off to who knew where!

The only good news in these chapters was the arrival of Henry Clerval to Ingolstadt, where his father had finally allowed him to study with his friend Frankenstein, and that Henry brings with him a letter from Elizabeth, a letter that Victor and Michelle were terribly excited to read.

Of Demons and Daemons

It was May, the very last month of school, and Jimmy was back in class. No students welcomed him. His scarring was repugnant, and many kids avoided him as if it were something catching. In some of the worst places, he was still wearing bandages. He enjoyed grossing out the girls by unwrapping himself, mummy-like.

Mrs. Terhart was also back in the classroom. She was gentle with him but firm about his treatment of other kids, and she promptly stopped this exhibitionism. She thought she noticed in those first few days Jimmy paying a lot of attention to Victor with looks and glares; it even appeared sometimes that Jimmy was following him whenever kids were moving about the room from activity to activity, walking to lunch, or going down to the library. She could tell that Victor was afraid. She couldn't figure out what trouble there was between them. There had been no incidents in the classroom, and she had heard no reports from the playground monitor. She would watch and listen. While she liked to think the best of everyone, she had more than a hunch that Jimmy was the kid teaching the other children on the playground the language of homophobia. She knew he was a tyrant, and she could also tell, sadly, that his accident had not changed him in any appreciable way.

Mrs. Terhart was not getting better, but she was determined to make it to the end of the year. She had developed an expertise at pretending she was not in pain, pretending she was strong and wide-awake, on top of her game. But when the students left, she deflated like a balloon and could barely move or think. She had lost weight and hair and had taken to wearing bandanas in lieu of wigs. The kids approved and thought it was a fashion statement, the kind adults would make, but a few of them understood. They had had family members on chemo or had seen things like this on television.

Mrs. Terhart's colleagues were astounded that she was working as much as she did and encouraged her to change her mind, but in the end, they supported her decision to work as long as she could work. The principal had even found resources to hire an assistant in her classroom who could help her plan, help her with student work, or take over at the drop of a hat if Mrs. Terhart became exhausted. It was clear to everyone that this was to help Mrs. Terhart continue with what she most wanted to do and not a way to make replacing her easy on the administration. Mrs. Terhart was thankful; she felt taken care of by her school.

Toward the end of silent reading time, Victor and Michelle began whispering back and forth.

"What's a daemon, Victor?"

Victor immediately pulled his dictionary out and was thumbing through the *D*'s. "Well, according to Webster—I know it's not as good as the Oxford—it means 'var of demon.' What does 'var' mean?"

"Variation, silly. *Daemon* means *demon*. That's a bad thing. Look up the word *demon*."

"Okay. *Demon*. Yeah, you're right. It's an evil spirit."

"Are there other definitions?"

"Yeah."

"Read them."

"Okay. 'An evil or undesirable emotion, trait, or state.'"

"Keep going, Victor. I can see there's more."

"Okay. 'An attendant power or spirit: Genius.' Wow. That's different. And it doesn't sound nearly as bad. Here's a fourth one: 'a supernatural being of Greek mythology intermediate between gods and men.' Hey, wasn't Prometheus one of those guys? Goodness. Here's another one! 'One that has unusual drive or effectiveness.' Hey, Shelley, how can the same word mean so many dang many things?"

"I think it's because the meanings of words change over time. In my Oxford, at home, it always tells you the origin of the word, and that gives you an idea of what it originally meant, and sometimes it's funny. I mean, sometimes a word, when you know where it began, becomes bigger, or truer. Like for example, the word *religion*."

"When people worship something, right? Like God or Jesus?"

"Yeah, but a long time ago the word meant simply to revere, to respect something a great deal. And now the word's meaning has changed so much that people don't even know what it means anymore. Religion is not about worship and stuff, but that's how we use it. And to me, if I were gonna have a religion, it'd be about respect, or just loving."

"Respect for what? Loving what?"

"I don't know," she said. Her eyes met Victor's, and for a moment they were both looking at themselves as reflections in the other child's eyes. Victor felt a shiver traveling up his spine and he put his hand on the top of his head to see if his hair was standing up. His hair was standing up.

Jimmy was across the room, fuming with anger and jealousy. His face was beet red. Mrs. Terhart had noticed this, and it frightened her. She could see the intensity beaming from him, and she tried not to blame him or hate him. She thought she understood now that he desperately wanted the kind of connection Victor and Michelle had developed so easily together, and then she felt sorry and wished there was something she could do for him. There was still time left in silent reading, but she wanted to interrupt the class early, if for no other reason than to distract Jimmy from his anger. In her head, she improvised a plan to have them group together in their pods of four and share with each other a few highlights from that day's reading. Jimmy had read nothing and would not participate, but the activity in the room and the immediate distraction of his own pod would keep him busy until recess, now only a matter of minutes away—only a matter of minutes before she could rest again. She announced the closure of today's silent reading period and gave them instructions for sharing in their pods something about what they had read.

Jimmy lost interest early in the conversation his pod members were having about their books, and he was angry still—but not at Victor and Michelle. Now he was very angry at the boys and girls in his group for being so smart and for being interested in something, and although he could not know it, he was ashamed of himself for having no way into the conversation, angry he was so inescapably dull. And then he looked at Mrs. Terhart as she observed the groups in the class and appeared to be taking notes on what they were doing. He found himself now inexplicably angry with his teacher. How stupid, he thought, to be so sick, to have so little time left on the planet and be spending it with a bunch of snotty kids. He found himself getting up from his chair, abandoning his group while Mrs. Terhart looked down at her desk and took notes, and he was walking around the classroom quietly, eventually arriving behind the teacher desk, behind Mrs. Terhart. It was not premeditated, but as he stood behind her trying to think of some way to expose her weakness, and perhaps, somehow, to prove to himself that it was all some elaborate ruse, Jimmy gave in to the first impulse he had and pulled the bandana from Mrs. Terhart's head. At her gasping, all activity was silenced, and the children were awe-struck, staring. She was mostly bald, but there were still tufts of hair, more like fuzz, in patches on her scalp. No one said a word. In that instant, Jimmy knew, or felt from some place inside of him that still knew the difference between good and evil, that he had done a terrible thing. But the other part of him was again the dominant characteristic, and to avoid appearing weak in any way, to avoid appearing like he did not know what he was doing, he continued down his destructive little path.

"Jesus, Mrs. Terhart, you look like Frankenstein's monster!"

A kid Victor did not know well, one Billy Fagelson, a quiet one, another of Jimmy's frequent targets for ridicule, stood up and shouted at the top of his voice: "And what do you look like—all wrinkly and shit, shriveled up like a raisin? No one's ever gonna wanna touch you, Jimmy."

Jimmy came charging across the room at the boy. Victor did not know what he was doing. He found himself between them, holding Jimmy back while he swung at Billy Fagelson. He was saying, "No, Jimmy," and it was with a sense, not of protecting Billy from harm, but of protecting

Jimmy from more trouble. He felt a need to straighten him out, but of course Jimmy could only see malice on Victor's part, another humiliation. And instead of overpowering Victor, as he could easily have done, he stepped away and spoke his little truth. "You die, Victor. When you're least expecting it, Frankenfag, I'll kill you, I swear, you faggot."

Her heart breaking, head throbbing, Mrs. Terhart could only plead, "Children!" It happened quickly. Before anyone got hurt, the assistant was bodily escorting Jimmy out of the room and to the office. Mrs. Terhart was crying. This is not how she wanted it to be—a fight in her classroom, the only physical one of her entire career, on one of the last days of the school year, on one of the last days of her life.

The principal expelled Jimmy, told him he would not be able to come back until the next school year, and called his father to pick him up immediately.

His dad was yelling at him the very instant Jimmy climbed inside the truck. It made very little impact on him, the yelling; it was the background noise of his life. But before the truck had traveled four blocks from the school, Jimmy received the first swat against his head from his father's right hand. Two blocks later came a smack against the ear. A half mile from home, Jimmy caught a closed fist that would blacken his eye. By the time the truck pulled into the driveway, there would be another four or five blows that Jimmy would not feel, because in his mind he had decided what he would do the minute he got into the house, and it made him numb to everything else in the world. It didn't take long. His father had sat down in front of the television within seconds of entering the house, and Jimmy had gone to his bedroom. He came back into the living room stealthily behind his father with the baseball bat he would use to kill him in just three swings: the first to knock him unconscious, and the last two to crush his skull.

A switch was thrown inside Jimmy's consciousness, perhaps as early as that fateful ride home in his father's truck. He didn't feel anything. And he didn't feel particularly inclined to do anything, either. He made no phone calls. He didn't leave the house. He changed the channel on the television, though, went into the kitchen to get a pop and a bag of chips, and sat down almost in the exact place on the couch where his father had been. Maybe later he would move the body, now crumpled up and still bleeding on the floor. Maybe he wouldn't. He had plenty of things to eat. He didn't need to go anywhere. And he wouldn't go anywhere for quite some time, so he would not know—would never know, perhaps—that only days later, Mrs. Terhart had taken a turn for the worse and was now in a hospital bed clear across town.

Of Last Rites

Justine and Mark were afraid they had made a terrible mistake in allowing Elizabeth to take Victor to the hospital where Mrs. Terhart lay dying. He was insistent, and they balanced one trauma against another—the grief he would feel at never being able to see her again against the grief of seeing her die. Ultimately, it came down to this: he could not be protected either way, and he needed to be able to choose for himself.

Elizabeth and Victor walked down the hospital hallways past room after room of sick and hurt people. Victor found himself thinking about this paradox: Dr. Frankenstein wanted at one and the same instant to help people and be worshipped by them. *"A new species would bless me as its creator and source; many happy and excellent natures would owe their being to me. No father could claim the gratitude of his child so completely as I should deserve theirs."* And Victor wondered about the doctors of his own time. Did they feel a similar conflict? Were they in it for others or for themselves? Did they feel god-like if they were able to cure someone of cancer, bring someone back from the dead, ease someone's pain? And were they, as Dr. Frankenstein was, leveled to the very depths of despair when they failed to realize their medical aspirations, when they misdiagnosed a patient, when they lost a person in a routine surgery, when they removed the wrong organ—or when they were helpless in the face of pancreatic cancer? How did they continue? Did they, do they, like Dr. Frankenstein did, become inconsolably depressed, physically sick themselves? Do they become voluntary amnesiacs? Victor was still very angry at Frankenstein's negligence. He imagined himself in Great-Granddaddy's predicament—barely able to move, lost in the wilderness without food, drink, or shelter, while his "parents" might have been mere blocks away trying desperately to forget his existence. Maybe we were, as the famous German poet had said, solitary creatures after all. But in the end, didn't we need other people to help us to learn to live with ourselves? Victor, while he did not have the language to ask these questions in this way, nevertheless felt bombarded by contradictions and opposites. And as he walked down this last hospital corridor in the cancer ward, counting down the room numbers, four, three, two, now one room away from Mrs. Terhart, he was already weeping, and he held his grandmother's hand. He would cure her if he could, not because she would worship him for it later, but because the world, the universe, seemed to require her presence in order to keep spinning. Everything, in Victor's estimation, would be somehow diminished without her.

Elizabeth and Victor were sitting in the hospital room by Mrs. Terhart's bed in two straight-back chairs. They sat there quietly for some time before even announcing their presence and being acknowledged. Mrs. Terhart had been sleeping, and they let her sleep until she started to come to, opening her eyes.

"Hello, Mrs. Terhart."

"Goodness," she spoke, soft and quiet. "Hello, Victor. What a tremendous surprise. And you've brought a friend."

"This is my grandma, Elizabeth."

"Grandma Elizabeth. It's so good to meet you."

"It's good to meet you, Mrs. Terhart."

"Call me June."

"We've heard so much about you from Victor."

"Victor is a special boy."

"Yes."

Victor was trying to be strong. He had to ask. "Mrs. Terhart, when will you come back to school?"

"Victor, I don't think I'll come back."

"Why not?" And he was starting to choke up, fighting the turmoil erupting in his throat and in his chest. "Why not?" he said again.

She said it deliberately, no hedging. "Victor, I am dying. I'm sorry I cannot tell you better news, but you deserve the truth about this."

"Okay," he said. "Okay," he said again. "Okay." Things became blurry to him. His head was awash. He wanted to say something. "I can't talk," he said.

"That's all right, Victor. You just sit there and be with me and your grandma."

He then laid his head in his grandmother's lap, as if he intended to sleep for a while. He closed his eyes and played a tape in his head of all of the memories he had of June Terhart before she was ill. It put him in a good place, and he was momentarily able to fight off his grief.

He could not know what was spinning inside of Grandma Elizabeth's heart. She was grappling with a terrible secret and simultaneously with a ferocious desire to protect Victor from suffering this particular loss. For a century she had fought a compulsion to use a terrible knowledge and skill against her better judgement. While Victor's head rested on his grandmother's lap, and after a long silence that was neither awkward nor embarrassing, Elizabeth began speaking the unspeakable to June Terhart.

"June, it is an honor to be here. Victor may not yet know it, but you are sharing with him a magnificent gift. Thank you for allowing us to see you." Then she spoke to the boy on her lap, "Victor, are you awake? Can you hear me speaking to your teacher?"

"Yes." He nodded.

"Good. I want you to listen closely now to what I'm saying to Mrs. Terhart, okay?"

"Yes."

"June, I know, because my daughter has told me about your earlier phone calls, probably when you had second graders, that Victor was telling some pretty crazy stories to his classmates."

"Yes, the monster thing, the Frankenstein thing."

"Exactly. The Frankenstein thing."

"Kids sure do have fabulous imaginations. Don't you ever lose that, Victor."

He did not respond.

"June," Elizabeth said. "I'm going to tell you something about those stories, and I want you to just be comfortable and relax, and don't forget to breathe."

"Yes?"

"These stories are true, June. Victor is truly the great-grandson of the monster created by his namesake, Victor Frankenstein, and I am the monster's daughter."

"That's a piece of fiction, dear. It's a novel by Mary Shelley."

"Yes, that is how it has come down to us in history, but it is, in truth, the story of Victor's family, the story of the beginnings of Victor's family. You are a part of that story now. There were, June, four other monsters, all dead now, and so the family is completely human—or, let us say, biologically no different from you. That is, they were all born of a mother's womb. I know this seems crazy to you. Please look at me. Look me in the eyes and see if you can detect any deception here. Let me hold your hand. Don't be afraid. This is the most important part. Victor, are you listening?"

"Yes."

June Terhart was holding Elizabeth's hand, and Victor was listening.

"June, I have the ability—"

Victor rose back up in his own seat.

"Despite my moral objections to the art that my father learned from his creator, I, too, know the art of reanimation."

"Grandma Elizabeth, you said—"

"Hold on, Victor. Don't speak, please."

Victor was silent.

"And in this case, June, in *your* case, I find good reason against my previous objections to use this skill now. I have the ability to bring you back after you die."

A long silence came into the room. June Terhart looked squarely into Elizabeth's eyes as she continued to speak. "Victor loves you very much. The community loves you very much. And I know your work could continue to enrich the lives of children. Modern doctors still do not understand many of the key mysteries of life and death. I understand them, June. I can bring you back. I can rid you of your cancer. I can make it possible for you to live another 150 years."

Fireworks went off in June Terhart's brain. Her gut reaction was anger—the audacity of this woman, the tastelessness of the joke, to mock her this way, and in front of a child. The sacrilege of playing games with another human being as she lay dying in a hospital bed, teasing out all of the vanity and insecurity and fear of a lifetime. But through these first anguished moments, she kept hold of Elizabeth's hand, and she kept her eyes fixed on Elizabeth's. Elizabeth's hand was warm, and there was something galvanizing about her gaze, absolutely crystal clear and steady. She felt like they were looking into each other's souls, the knower and the known, an intimacy as deep as any she had ever formed manifested in a single moment. This Grandma Elizabeth was a beautiful woman, a deep, intelligent spirit, and she was not crazy. She was not playing a cruel joke, and she was not lying. But this having to die first in order to be cured, June Terhart suspected, was wrong, somehow. And even if it were possible, and she now believed that it was, it was the wrong time, and she was the wrong person. In her mind and in her body, she had let go of this life, had embraced her imminent death, had welcomed it. And the thought of another 150 years, miraculous as that was, was somehow unappealing. Her professional life had been rewarding beyond measure, but also exhausting, and throughout the rest of her life was a catalogue of sufferings: the adultery of her first husband, the ensuing divorce, her infertility, the death of the second husband, the loss of her parents, and the weariness that set in, even before the diagnosis. No, she could not do that, any of that, again and again and again.

"You just tell me if you can do it—if you want to live, if you want me to save you, to bring you back."

"No," June Terhart said. " I don't want that."

And Victor sobbed.

Victor sobbed and laid his head back down in Elizabeth's lap while she continued to hold June Terhart's hand and to smile at her. She said, "All right, June. All right."

Of the End of the Fourth Grade

Jimmy had gotten used to the smell of his father's rotting carcass but grew tired of looking at it. He had the presence of mind to finally do something, and one early morning, when it was dark and the neighborhood was sleeping, he dragged the body outside and buried it in the yard as he'd remembered burying dead pets. The burial was difficult, strenuous work, and it helped only a little to exorcise the image of his dad's dead body lying around the house. Even after he was gone and the smell started to dissipate a little, he could still see him in his mind's eye: hitting, grousing, cursing, bleeding, falling, and dying stupidly on the living room carpet. Days afterward, trying to think of something more cheerful, he realized that it was the last day of school before summer break, and he was concerned suddenly with keeping his word. He traveled on foot with a baseball bat still mottled with the dried blood of his father to a distant part of his neighborhood. Jimmy waited for Victor in a culvert he knew he would pass on the way home from his bus stop. Jimmy wasn't scared or nervous. He had a job to do.

The last week of school had been dark indeed for Victor. Mrs. Terhart was dead. He wept inconsolably for an entire weekend, stopping only when Michelle came by on Sunday evening for a visit. And the last week of school was torturous and confusing. Here was this new teacher, talking about Mrs. Terhart as if she knew her, talking about the fourth grade as if she were there the whole time, and it made Victor angry. And it was impossible not to think about Mrs. Terhart. To start with, the school counselors kept encouraging them all to keep talking about their feelings. And in that classroom, everything reminded him of her—the smell of crayons, the feel of a pair of scissors in his hand, Elmer's glue, the way it dried almost clear on a piece of red construction paper, the pencil sharpener, how it always sharpened a pencil perfectly, the view of the trees and the field of the playground out the classroom window, and that desk, that huge, oaken, beautiful desk where another teacher was sitting. All of these things brought Mrs. Terhart front and center in Victor's mind. Michelle had convinced him that this was all a very good sign. It meant that he would never forget his teacher, and she would thus be always with him. They muddled through and were compliant and sad, and the whole week, instead of an exhilarating stretch before a three-month vacation, was dirge-like, slow and gloomy. The playground was not playful; the grass was not green; the trees were not leafy and inviting; the sunshine, even, was somehow diminished. The only thing that remained unchanged for Victor—no, perhaps now it became an even greater prize than ever—was his friendship with Michelle.

As a misguided but well-intentioned final exam on the last day of school, the children were asked to make drawings representing their learning, growth, and memories of the fourth grade year. After making some pictures representing math concepts of three digit multiplication and long division, some illustrations of some stories he remembered reading, (especially the one about the boy and his dogs), some diagrams of science concepts he remembered, and a little drawing of a boy learning to ignore bullies, he began drawing a picture of Mrs. Terhart and immediately began weeping. He felt that he might die from it, from this grief. Michelle sat next to him, squeezed his arm, and began making good-natured little cracks about his drawing. "Victor, her hips were not that wide. She'll be mad at you for making her look so chunky." Victor laughed. And then, despite the risk of derision from her classmates, she actually put her arm around him and gave him a hug. "She's gone from us, Victor. But there are still good things if you just think of them."

They sat together quietly, Michelle holding Victor's hand under the table at which they sat, the room full of children abuzz around them in the last minutes of the last day of their fourth grade year. And moments later, outside the school, before Michelle walked to her bus and Victor walked to his, she held his hand once more, looked right into his eyes, and told him she loved him. "Remember, Victor. There is still beauty in the world." And those were the words, on this last day of school, that he was repeating to himself as he got off the bus and began to walk home, his backpack full of treasures, of remembrances of a school year and a teacher he would never forget, and his heart pounding with happiness and love for a fourth grade girl he named Shelley. "There is still beauty in the world. There is still beauty in the world."

There was a flurry of activity behind him—the whooshing of the leaves of a brittle bush, an animal perhaps, a dog digging for a squirrel or a cat hiding in the brush—but what made Victor turn around finally was this high-pitched, other-worldly moaning or wailing, the voice of some child in anguish or pain. It took Victor some time to cipher out what he was seeing. It was a monster—no, a boy—running toward him, arms up over his head, waving something wildly in the air: a big stick—no, a baseball bat. Victor recognized the scarred and disfigured face of Jimmy, and he was instantaneously terrified. He turned and ran. Jimmy caught up easily. Victor felt the familiar loss of breath that came with the enormous pressure at his back, and he was flying. He spilled into a neighbor's yard, not four houses away from home. Jimmy, wanting to prolong his pleasure in attacking Victor, first grabbed at Victor's backpack as he lay in the grass and pulled it away from him. He opened it up and deliberately dumped its contents into the yard and started kicking them around, sometimes picking things up and ripping them in half in his hands with great glee and exuberance. Valentine cards Victor had kept, stories and poems he'd written, pictures he'd drawn, notes on *Frankenstein*—all of it flying every which way around this yard and around Victor's head as he tried to get up to stop him. He managed to stand. And then Jimmy was wielding the bat as if he actually intended to use it against him. There was a pain in Victor's arm unlike anything in his wildest nightmares as the first blow landed squarely against his flesh. And then there was darkness, and he could feel himself falling. And then, only moments later, he was flying again.

When the neighbor, who had been away, came home, she called 911 in hysterics. This is what the paramedics and the police found when they arrived: school work scattered all over Betty Litson's yard and the empty backpack in the grass, all belonging to a boy named Victor who lived four houses down. And in the middle of it all, a fourth grader lying chest, pubis, and thigh down to the grass, while, grotesquely, his face looked up to the blue June sky. Neck broken, dead to the world, lay a child known in the neighborhood as Jimmy the gasoline boy. Victor was not home, and there was no sign of him. The first thing that crossed Officer Babbit's mind was that the missing boy killed this other kid. But there was no way, he thought, a child could be strong enough or brutal enough to kill another child this way, by turning his head completely around where it sat on his shoulders. Not a chance. But it was clear enough that if the boy named Victor didn't kill the boy named Jimmy, he at least was present when it happened. He would have been the only witness to this heinous crime. Subsequently, the police found themselves at Jimmy's address discovering other grisly surprises—a home in complete disrepair and squalor, evidence of another violent struggle, and a dead body inexpertly buried in the backyard with the carcasses of household pets gone years before.

Part Two

Of The Monster That Got Away

Earlier by more than a century, Adam had traversed a great tract of land before finding his prospective son-in-law, his own creation, his daughter's bridegroom, rejected and dismissed by her—not dead, in fact, but living among a tribe of Natives, speaking their language, adopting their culture, working, astonishingly enough, as a shaman of sorts. He adapted so quickly, and it was imminently obvious to Adam how advanced this creature actually was: the ugliest of monsters that had ever walked the earth with the brains of the most sophisticated scholar. Adam had not decided what he would do when he found him, but it didn't take him long to decide. This was far better for the creature than life in his own family would have been. There were apologies, half-hearted efforts at reconciliation, and some dismissive talk about his daughter, Elizabeth, whom the creature was clearly better off without ("the naughty, ungrateful baggage"), and a promise was made with only the lips and none of the heart to help him out if he were ever in need. The offer was completely superfluous, as the monster was obviously and completely self-sufficient. And despite the creature's advanced intelligence, he was not any more honest with Adam than Adam was honest with him. While feigning disinterest, the truth of the matter was that he had loved Elizabeth at first glance, loved her still deeper in their first meeting, and loved her still deeper, as thoroughly and as stupidly as is possible for a monster to love a woman, as she rejected him, told him she could never have him. And he waited some 120 years before he knew it was time to find her again. He wished no harm to come to the child, but he knew the absence of Victor would get Elizabeth's attention better than anything could. He certainly did not envision snapping that other little bastard's neck—he just got in the goddamned way—and that boy stinking of gasoline was in the process of damaging his precious cargo. In fact, he knew it was true—if he had been a moment later, Victor would now be dead.

His was a deep, large, unfamiliar voice. "No broken bones. That's good."

"Great-Grandaddy?" It was the first thing Victor said when he opened his eyes and found himself lying on a cot inside of what appeared to be a large, open, rustic log cabin, while this enormous creature dressed his wound and rubbed a kind of salve on his bare arm over a nasty bruise left by the blow of a baseball bat.

"Your great-grandaddy has been dead over a hundred years, Victor."

"Then ..." He was thinking it through, trying to find a solution to the query on his own and stalling.

"Great-Grandaddy, no. I might have been your *Grandaddy*, though. But then you might not have been born."

"I don't understand."

"There's no need to understand. Not yet. You rest. Relax. Don't be afraid. I won't hurt you."

"Jimmy," Victor said. "What happened to Jimmy?"

"Jimmy. He was a different story."

"He would have killed me."

"As sure as I'm sitting here."

"I'm not afraid," said Victor.

"I didn't think you would be. Rest. Sleep some, if you like."

"Can we go home? Will you take me home?"

"No," said the monster, and he turned away from him. "I can't do that. Not yet."

Victor did not press the issue. He did not have the inner resources.

In silence, Victor lay on this cot, a bundle of blankets under and over him, looking out at this giant now sitting on a cushion on the cabin floor with his back to him. He was very still. For a moment, Victor imagined he was looking at a statue, and his heavy eyes kept blinking. He did not want to fall asleep. He wondered if perhaps he was already asleep. But then he remembered the feeling of being followed; he remembered perilous nightmares; he remembered Grandma Elizabeth's stories. And then he thought he knew. "You're supposed to be dead."

"So are you, young man."

"No, I mean, I was told that you were dead."

"Surprise."

"And you're not so terrible looking."

"Well, thank you very much indeed."

"I was told you were a hideous monster."

Yes, the monster was ugly, but not in the way Victor had imagined it, not in the way he dreamed it would be, and finally, most significantly in Victor's mind, not in the way Elizabeth had described it. He wasn't elephant man ugly, not even monster movie ugly. He was gigantic and brutish, yes, disproportioned in places, scarred, yes, and unhandsome in the extreme, but no one seeing him on a busy city street would scream or run away. Stare, maybe. People would stare at this monster, but they would not run away. Human beings of the twenty-first century had grown accustomed to a certain level of ugliness. Victor was exhausted, and despite efforts to remain focused on this strange individual sitting next to him and an aching desire to know where he was and when he could go home, he allowed himself to close his eyes and fall asleep.

Victor's household was in absolute panic and despair. Mark was in constant contact with the authorities. Justine sobbed and made phone calls. Elizabeth was uncharacteristically silent. There was very little any of them could do. Victor's face would be everywhere—on the news, on TV and in print; on fliers in the hands of every police officer in the city; and eventually even on milk cartons. After that, it was just a question of waiting. Neighbors came to comfort and take care and help wherever they could, but the family said thank you and turned them away.

Police officers asked the family questions. Did Victor hate Jimmy? No, Victor never spoke of Jimmy. As far as they were aware, the two boys did not know each other. Officer Babbit, after a little digging around, had found out that the boys did indeed know each other, that, according to everyone he spoke to, Jimmy was a playground bully of an especially nasty stripe, and that Victor was often his target. Victor, despite the fact that he never spoke of these things, had reason to hate Jimmy and even a possible motive toward violence. The family protested. Victor was incapable of hatred—and of violence. It just was not part of his constitution. He might protect himself, but his most likely mode of self-preservation would be to run away; he could never do something like that to another boy. He would not even entertain the thought, they said. "We just have to ask," Officer Babbit had said. "Victor has no record at school of any violent behavior or tendencies. His first and third grade teachers and the principal all speak very highly of him. We believe it's unlikely that Victor did this. Again, we just have to ask. We've got to explore every possibility."

And there was a possibility, a piece of information, that was not forthcoming from Officer Babbit. It was just too early to say anything else but that they were following some leads. But from random people in the community, every once in a hundred times, they would find someone who would describe a strange man in the neighborhood they had never seen before—a tall, large, ugly, and "retarded-looking" man skulking around the school. He had very little to go on, but Babbitt knew that this was his man.

"Why have you taken me away from my home?"

"I wanted to meet you."

"You're lying."

"Yes. Although, meeting you is a bonus, I suppose."

"Why did you take me away from home?"

"To protect you from Jimmy."

"But you killed Jimmy, didn't you?"

"Then I took you away to protect myself from the authorities."

"You're lying. This gets you into even more trouble."

"Yes."

"Why did you do it?"

"To get somebody's attention."

"Phone calls are good." Victor was surprised by his own courage. "Letters—that could work. There's always e-mail."

There was silence then.

Victor ventured forth. "Whose attention do you want?"

"Elizabeth. I want your Grandma Elizabeth's attention."

"I would say you've probably got it. Only—and I'm just a kid—but I'm guessing that her attention right now is on me, not you.

"Exactly."

"And when she does find me, she'll be very angry at you. Is that what you want?"

"No."

"I think that's what you'll get."

"Sometimes anger is the best you can do. Sometimes anger is better than nothing at all." But already he had begun to doubt the wisdom of his strategy.

"I still think you should have just picked up the phone."

"You're a funny boy."

"I'm not trying to be funny."

"Maybe not. But you made a joke. And for all you know, I could be planning to eat you alive."

"You're not planning that."

"I cannot tell you what I am planning," the monster said, and it was because he did not know.

"I'm a little bit scared now."

"Okay. That's all right. Don't be."

Later, Victor noticed darkness and the desert cold, and he had no idea what time it was. But he thought of Michelle and immediately started to sob. The idea that he might never see her again shook him somewhere deep within his bones, and he was shaking and sobbing. He thought he could brave the loss of his own family better.

"What is it, little man?"

Victor could not answer. He felt a big hand on his forehead, rough and warm.

"You're not feverish."

And there was a moment when this creature, touching Victor's skin, watching him shake, and listening to him moan, caught a vibration of something familiar, and immediately he knew. "You are in love."

Victor said nothing, but in his convulsions of grief, he was nodding his head.

"I fell in love once, and every other experience of love after has paled in comparison. And it's not about carrying a torch—well, yes, actually, it is exactly about carrying a torch."

Victor took a deep breath in between sobs. He pictured in his mind's eye the concluding scene from the Boris Karloff film, torches and windmills. He was confused, and he asked, "Carrying a torch?"

"It's a metaphor. People who have difficulty letting go of other people, even after the possibility of being with them is extinguished, are said to be carrying a torch—you know, keeping a light burning, hoping against hope. It's total lunacy."

Victor thought of Dennis, then Mrs. Terhart, and then Michelle. "Then why do they do it?"

"Listen, little man—what do you think *you're* doing if you are weeping for a loved one?"

"I'm not carrying a torch, you. I'm not hoping against hope. Whatever that means, I'm not doing it. The only reason I can't be with Shelley is because you're keeping me from her."

"Shelley is her name?"

"Michelle."

"Clever. Okay. Maybe you're right. I'm the one with the torch. The ugly one with the torch. Go back to sleep, little man."

"First tell me two things."

"Okay."

"Who did you fall in love with?"

"Elizabeth. One hundred and twenty years ago."

"That's a long time to carry a torch."

"What's the second thing?"

"What's your name?"

"They called me Horace. Friends call me Pinky."

It was morning. Light flooded the inside of the cabin through large, well-appointed wood windows, but it was cool. A breeze blew through the screen of a double-hung sash. Victor woke up with the question on his tongue, and he spoke it before even placing its intended audience anywhere in the room. Out into the air he spoke, "Why don't you just go to her?"

"It seems so simple, doesn't it?" A voice came to Victor, but he could not see the speaker. Was he still asleep and dreaming? His eyes were open, and he looked toward the ceiling of the cabin and at the massive fir support beams that held it in place. It was getting warm. A ceiling fan spun.

Victor spoke again. "She may not feel the same way she did then."

"She will feel the same way," said the voice.

"I think she's lonely."

"I have murdered a child," said the voice. "She will hate me."

"I think she is dying," Victor said, and that settled that.

Barricaded in her bedroom for two days running, Michelle had had no contact with the outside world since the news had come from Victor's parents that he was missing. She had cried herself into several stupors. She would not eat. She made a fetish out of every item in her possession that had any connection whatsoever to Victor. There were drawings he had made her, a couple of portraits, uncanny in their likeness to the image she saw in the mirror. There were valentine cards, notes, and a jacket he had loaned her one time when she was cold on the playground that she had never given back. She smelled him on it, and she kept smelling him. She remembered how he commented once about how wonderful she smelled and how silly that seemed to her then—but how absolutely poignant it was to her now that she was holding something of his with his own unique smell all over it. And there was her copy of *Frankenstein,* which she could not bear to read outside of Victor's company.

Three days had gone by, and from her seemingly unshakeable silence, finally Elizabeth awoke into a kind of agitated panic. She paced the room. She looked out the living room window over and over again, expecting to see Victor walking up the drive, or, in darker moments, expecting to see the police car without a passenger and the officer walking soberly to the door to deliver the news. "I can't stand this waiting," Elizabeth said. "It is unbearable."

"Mom, there's nothing we can do. We can only wait," Justine said.

"Waiting is a fool's game," she said. "Fuck waiting. I'm going out. I will find him."

"Mother," said Mark, "what makes you think you'll have better luck than the people who are trained to do these things? For God's sake, don't be stupid. If he's out there they will find him."

"I will find him first," she said, and by that time she had gathered up her purse, a jacket or two, and her car keys, and she was out the door.

"Jesus H. Christ," Justine said.

And at the end of the driveway as she was backing out, Elizabeth saw her by the mailbox. Forlorn, face covered with tears enough to drown a fully grown woman, and a suitcase by her side, Michelle stood at the mailbox and watched Elizabeth as she backed the Subaru out of the driveway. Elizabeth stopped immediately and rolled down the window. "Hey there, little one. What are you doing?"

At first Michelle could not answer. Her lips moved as if to speak, but no words came forth. Finally, she told Elizabeth that she did not know what she was doing. "I want Victor back," she said, "but I thought that if I could not be with him, I could be with you, maybe, or Justine and Mark, or, just to be in his house again."

And as Justine watched from the kitchen window, Elizabeth opened the door. "Get in the car, Shelley," she said.

Hours later, as Michelle's parents were scrambling to track their own child down, it seemed to all concerned parties that some stranger had kidnapped Victor, and then Grandma Elizabeth had kidnapped Victor's girlfriend.

Of Lost and Found

For hours Elizabeth drove or walked around her town with this fourth grader in tow, knocking on doors, stopping people in parks and in stores and on the sidewalk, asking anyone she found at any place and at any time if they had seen the boy in the photo. The answer was always no, accompanied by either a quick walk away by those who were strangers to the family and couldn't be bothered or a sad, empathetic look and maybe a gentle touch or hug from people who knew the family but had no information.

They stopped for the night at a cheap motel, farther away from home than Elizabeth had intended to travel, but neither of them could sleep. They felt useful and found comfort in each other's company. Even though their first efforts to find Victor had failed, they still felt like this was a far better thing than waiting around and wasting precious time that could make all the difference in the world. They did not speak about their deepest fears. Michelle imagined some kind of slave camp for little boys and girls or a sweatshop of some kind from which Victor would never return. Elizabeth's thoughts were darker. She feared that Victor had been murdered like that other boy, or worse yet, tortured and murdered, or still worse, sexually abused, tortured, and murdered, and these nightmarish thoughts were unbearable to hold onto for long. So she distracted herself and Michelle with a game of Scrabble they had checked out at the front office.

Michelle was winning by way of chancing upon all the right letters to spell words that described Victor. Sweet. Quiet. Good. Smart. Elizabeth was having an unusually terrible time concentrating. She felt like sometimes she did not even recognize the letters on the tiles. "What the hell is this thing, this funny shape?" she found herself asking.

"That's an *H*, silly," said the little girl. She followed with the question burning in her head. "Elizabeth? Who would want to take Victor away?"

"The world is full of sick people."

"I don't understand. Ah, here's a good one. Look, I get to use the *Q* again." She placed tiles on the board that spelled out *quizy*.

"That's not how you spell queasy."

"No, it's quizy. As opposed to testy."

"That's very funny, sweetheart, but it's not a word."

"Okay," and she took the tiles back. "Elizabeth? Is it true that your father was Frankenstein's monster?"

"Yes, Michelle. It's true."

"And is it true that he built monsters for his children as husbands and brides?"

"Yes. That's true."

"Why did he have to do that?"

"Adam believed that making a new monster for his human children would be better than mixing with others in society or breeding with the natives. I understand why he did it, but I think he was wrong to do it."

"But Victor said you offered to bring Mrs. Terhart back."

"That was wrong of me. I shouldn't have done that. I wasn't thinking. But it turned out all right in the end. I was desperate to make Victor's sadness go away."

"I understand that. But could you really have done it? Could you have brought her back?"

Elizabeth did not respond.

"It seems like you'd be doing something bad to make somebody else feel good. Elizabeth? What happened to the monsters your daddy made?"

"It only proves my point, Shelley. My brothers both died in World War I, and their monster-brides, in utter, absolute despair, took their own lives, together, at the same time—they agreed to poison themselves rather than make the effort that the rest of us were already making to integrate into the society. And they were right—not to kill themselves, I mean, but they knew that they would never be able to have normal lives in Phoenix, where the rest of us were moving."

"Tell me about the other one."

"Which?"

"The monster your daddy made for you."

"Oh, Shelley. Can we not talk about that?"

Michelle could see the exasperation on Elizabeth's face, and she only thought for a split second about pressing on. "Okay. You don't have to tell me."

"I'm sorry," Elizabeth said. She thought of the promise she'd made to herself never to keep secrets from children, and the hypocrisy reared its ugly head at her. She went forward. "It's a terrible story, Shelley." Adam, from the search for his most recent creation, had come back to the village empty-handed, saying that the monster was dead. Elizabeth knew, however, simply by looking into her father's eyes that this was only a partial truth. It was as if God was speaking into her ear, a result of her imagined culpability in the event of the monster's exile. "I believe Adam murdered his monster, murdered his own son," Elizabeth said to Michelle.

"I don't believe that," said the little girl, and the Scrabble game was over.

They were canvassing the neighborhood the entire next morning and into the afternoon until the young girl was exhausted beyond the ability to speak another word or walk another step, and Elizabeth decided to take the girl home and to go home herself. Mark, goddamn him, was right. She was tired, and this fruitless search had helped nothing, had solved no problems, did not bring Victor any closer to home.

Michelle was asleep as Elizabeth drove the Subaru down the last stretch of road toward Victor's home, planning to stop there briefly to tell Justine and Mark to call ahead to the girl's parents so they knew she was safe and on her way. And as she drove down El Mesa Drive, with oleander bushes and Russian olive trees flanking the car on either side and the sun flickering down through the leaves and into the car, six, five, four houses from the boy's home, she saw something that simultaneously frightened her almost to death and thrilled her to unbelievable heights of joy. A tall, gigantic man walked down the sidewalk carrying a small child in his arms. She knew immediately it was a boy and knew immediately after that it was Victor, but quickly the joy was replaced in her mind by a fierce protectiveness. She slammed on the brakes parallel to the giant and the boy (Michelle, asleep, would have flown through the windshield had she not been buckled in), and Elizabeth was in the street, shouting with all of her strength and courage from ten feet away and pointing her finger as if she were holding a gun. "Put the boy down, you son of a bitch. Put the boy down!"

The big man immediately complied and Victor was running to his grandmother's arms. "Grandma! Grandma Elizabeth. It's okay. I'm okay. He hasn't hurt me. He's a friend!"

The boy was safe, uninjured in her arms and her face was buried in his hair and she was crying and she wasn't looking at the man. "Oh Jesus. God. I'm sorry. I didn't know what to think. I didn't know. We've been so worried and I didn't even ask myself why someone who had hurt him would be taking him home. What happened, Victor? Who is this man?" And now she finally looked at the figure that stood on the sidewalk in perfect stillness. "Who are you? My God. I think. No. I think I know you. My memory has not been good these four days. Oh my. My God."

And she had let Victor go, and he was walking toward the parked car in the middle of the street where a fourth grade girl named Shelley stood watching and waiting. They held each other there, sobbing in the street, the sun flickering down at them in the shade of a row of lemon trees.

Of Reunions

Mark had become a believer. Horace, Pinky, had shown him the scars, the places where limbs were added, where organs were inserted, where surgical corrections were made, where life had been infused. And Mark, a history buff, was astounded at the level of detail Pinky could unveil about his experiences over the last 120 years, details Justine had simply not bothered to reveal to him and that seemed (unfairly, in retrospect) ludicrous coming from his mother-in-law. Justine attributed this to some hidden sexism within Mark's character, that he would much sooner believe a man about such things than his own wife or her mother. Mark was embarrassed but refused to take responsibility for chauvinistic behavior, pointing to Horace's scars as the evidence that finally convinced him. He'd never seen anything like it, and neither his wife nor his mother-in-law had evidence like that.

The family was so elated to get Victor safely back into their home and so full of gratitude to this long-lost relative that it took quite some time for them to find the nasty bruise on Victor's arm and then to approach the subject of Horace's involvement. How exactly had he come across Victor, and how had he known who he was? Victor jumped into the fray before Horace could speak and told a relatively convincing tale about Jimmy stealing his school things as he got off the bus, hitting him on the arm with a big stick, and running away, and Victor, in pursuit, lost him and his way back home.

"But Victor," Justine said. "Your things were found in the Litson's front yard with Jimmy's body."

"Well, like I said, I got lost. Jimmy must have doubled back. I don't know why he would have put my things there or what happened to him. Jimmy's never been to our house—maybe he thought that's where I lived. And maybe somebody attacked him there."

"Okay, then. Let's recap. You get lost running after Jimmy. You're roaming around the neighborhood for days? And this man, our long-lost—" She paused, unsure what to call him. "At any rate, this man, who Elizabeth hasn't seen for 120 years, suddenly shows up and takes you home? Victor, dear. You're tired and you need some rest, maybe. And when you feel better, you can think more clearly, perhaps, about what has happened. It's important, Victor. Officer Babbit will want to know. There's a boy that's been killed."

"I know that, Mother."

Elizabeth had pulled Horace out through the sliding glass patio door and into the backyard garden, a masterfully choreographed arrangement of eucalyptus, agave, aloe vera, and Mexican Bird of Paradise. It was an uncharacteristically cool day at eighty-six degrees. They stood together, not speaking, for quite some time. Elizabeth was sizing him up. Horace tried not to stare and wrestled against several conflicting impulses.

She could not read him and noticed that when she looked directly at him, he averted his eyes. Either he was hiding something or he was painfully shy or both. She would have to speak.

"Walk with me," she said and moved out into the yard among the verbena and bear grass, slowly, thoughtfully moving over the stone pathway through the garden.

"Elizabeth, it is so good to see you again. I am beside myself. I am finding it hard to know what to say. Only that it's good to see you."

"We all thought you were dead."

"Yes. And I did nothing for a century to let you know otherwise."

"I'm glad. I mean, I'm glad you're not dead. I had imagined the worst possible scenario."

"Yes. And you helped Victor to believe I was more monster than monster."

"It was all in good fun. I never imagined we would see you again. He loves the stories."

"He's confused now about how to tell the real ones from the made-up ones. And now he thinks you lied to him."

"Who's lying now, Horace?"

"Please, call me Pinky."

"That boy in there is hiding something. You killed this Jimmy kid, didn't you?"

He did not respond, and in effect answered the question for her.

"Shit," she said. "What happened, Horace?"

"This Jimmy would have murdered Victor. He hit him with a baseball bat, and he was swinging for his head when I grabbed him."

"My God," she said, weeping. "My little Victor. This little boy killed his father the same way. He was one sick little fucker."

"Yes, he was, but abused, wretchedly abused." He wanted to hold her. He was frozen there, watching her weep.

"Why didn't you just stop the boy? Why did you kill him?"

He could not answer the question.

"Horace," she said. "You know what this means?"

"If I'm caught, I'll go to jail."

"Jail? You'll be on death row."

"It would have been worth it. Victor's life is worth the lives of a thousand kids like Jimmy."

"I don't know if I like the sound of that. I mean, I agree. But imagine rounding up a thousand Jimmys and breaking their necks."

"You know what I mean. It's a figure of speech. All I'm saying is that I think it would be worth it to have saved Victor's life. And to have been able to see you again. I feel like I've lived long enough. I could die right now in your gaze, happily."

"This is too much. I have to lay down."

Elizabeth abruptly turned away from him, walked back into the house, and left him standing by the eucalyptus in the garden. And he stood still and silent and breathed deeply for several minutes before deciding he would tell Justine and Mark the story.

It's easy to discern the nature of the quandary in which Victor's parents found themselves. Justine and Mark had their beloved son back. They were aware that this man Horace had saved their child from a brutal and early death by killing the perpetrator of the deed, a young boy who had murdered his father days or weeks before, leaving himself alone in the world. An orphan, he would spend the rest of his youth, when caught, in some sort of detention center, a boy who would stand little chance of ever living what most folks would call a normal life, who would probably end up committing another crime, if not one right after the other, and who would most likely spend the rest of his life in and out of correctional institutions, unloved, uncared for, a blight on society, a miserable human being. But then again—who could know these things? In all of the powers of knowledge and science and philosophy inherited by this family through the strangest and most miraculous of histories, no one, from Dr. Frankenstein on, had the power to know the future well enough to make reliable predictions. The doctor was correct—the monsters would come to the new world. He was absolutely on the mark that somehow they would end up in the dry heat of a desert land. But he could not, in his wildest imagination, have dreamt of the end result of his corruption, of the goodness and love imbued in this little boy, of his namesake, Victor.

They had come to the conclusion that Horace was not a danger to them, that he was not a killer of children. But he was, as a result of this one act that saved their boy by sacrificing another, a liability. It was not the family's place, Justine felt, to make a call about the relative worth of one boy's life against another's—although, if it were up to them, there could only be one choice. If Horace stayed with them, they could not protect him. All they could do, whether he stayed or moved on, would be to feign ignorance of his culpability.

"It's good of you. I don't blame you. I expect nothing less," the monster said to Justine and Mark.

Mark said it, something that had been on his mind and probably on the minds of both Justine and Elizabeth: a question about the time. "Why did you wait four days to bring him back?"

"I was frightened. I was confused. I did not know what to do. I wanted more than anything to meet you and be with you, but I was afraid that I would be treated as I have been treated throughout my life, by my father and by most of the communities in which I tried to live—as a monster. I have had my share of blind men who cared for me, but like your grandfather, Justine, the majority of people who have eyes but refuse to make good use of them reject me, treat me like a freak, hunt me down for being ugly and afraid. And that rejection was terrifying to me, even as it is the oldest feeling I know."

And Justine said, "You are welcome here, Horace."

"Please," he said, "call me Pinky."

Grandma Elizabeth, in her daughter and son-in-law's bedroom, drifting in and out of a kind of fitful sleep, was dreaming or remembering something from a long time ago. Days after the news had come of the death of her brothers on the western front, she had gone to visit their wives. Finding the first home empty, she walked down the dirt road to the other, knocking on the door for what seemed like an eternity, knocking, knocking. Finally, she tried the front door, found it unlocked, and walked into the desert log cabin her brother William had built for his monster wife—identical to the one Ernest had built for his. There were no children for either brother; their wives had proved infertile. And then they both went off, as if punishing their wives or themselves, to a war neither of them fully understood, about which neither of them felt any passion.

The cabin was silent, and when Elizabeth called there was no answer. There were only three rooms, a large and open dining and living space with a brick fireplace and a washroom situated just to the left of a bedroom, so it only took a minute to find them, apparently taking a nap together on the bed William had made with his own hands. They looked peaceful, Elizabeth thought, and she imagined that they had been mourning together and that this had turned into a sorrowful sleeping. She saw tears on both their faces. Elizabeth sat on the bed next to them, and in a moment of tenderness uncharacteristic of her behavior toward her brothers' wives, she reached for the hand of Ernest's bride, held it for a moment, and finding it very cold, put her fingers on the monster's pulse and found nothing. She did the same for William's wife with the same result. They both lay dead, an empty bottle of arsenic on the nightstand.

And on that day, one thing became crystal clear to Elizabeth. She was utterly alone. Her parents had both been dead now for years, leaving her brothers and their wives her only family, and now all of them had gone in one fell swoop. She felt immediately at once betrayed by and a traitor to her own family. They had all left her alone, had been completely selfish, and had shown no consideration for her situation, but at the same time, she had withheld acceptance, withheld her love from them—from her brothers at the start for their encouragement of the monster making, from their monster brides for what they represented to her, from the creature that was made as her husband, who she imagined was then murdered by his creator, her own father. But in this present waking dream, she saw or remembered herself moving away from the village, leaving every vestige of her family behind her, entering what passed for civilization in early twentieth century Phoenix, finding her way into society, and finding love several times over in one man after another, and eventually in a child she named Justine after one of her father's earliest victims. And she had a sense the whole time that every once in a while there may have been a monster watching her and waiting to eventually give her another opportunity to right a wrong, to make something good of a bad thing. And there came, too, an impulse and then a drive to learn all of what she could of the art, making a vow to herself never to use what she still considered the dark science of reanimation. She was asleep now, and this was a dream she was having, standing in front of a monster named Horace and speaking in a whisper she could feel in her throat, words forming on her lips. "Forgive me," she felt herself say, and she could see the monster smiling.

Of Honesty and Confession

After a brief adjustment period in which Michelle became used to and comfortable with Horace, Victor and Michelle wasted no time getting back to *Frankenstein*, inviting the giant to listen in on their readings. So in the library, while Horace looked on from the Morris settee, Michelle and Victor reread out loud of Dr. Frankenstein's anguish over his terrible accomplishments, of the disappearance of his creation, of a nervous fever—in effect, a psychological breakdown—that kept him isolated for months, of Henry Clerval, his only attendant, nursing him back to health while keeping his condition a secret from the family. And finally, Victor and Michelle read ahead to a letter Clerval discovers, unopened, from Dr. Frankenstein's dear adopted "cousin" Elizabeth, Victor's grandmother's namesake.

Listening to this young girl read Elizabeth's words out loud had a strange effect on Horace. It was not *his* Elizabeth—but there was a quality to her written voice and to the way, perhaps, that Michelle interpreted it that reminded him of the woman he had loved so long and with whom he had just now finally been reunited. He entertained few illusions about what this reunion might bring about; he convinced himself, for the most part, that it was enough to be close to her, to hear her voice, and to actually have the opportunity to know the woman he had fallen madly in love with after only one or two very short conversations 120 years ago. He thought, initially, that this familiarization with her might break the spell;

there would no longer be any mystery to her, and she would fall from his idealized pedestal. So far, though, his new acquaintance with her, as brief as it was to this point, was only causing his love to deepen. And this letter of hers, but not hers, came into his ears as a wonder, as he imagined and had imagined before that this is how she would speak to him if she felt for him the way this Elizabeth felt for her Dr. Frankenstein.

Elizabeth's letter, besides being a statement of her concern and affection and an urgent plea for the doctor to write home, was mostly small talk about family, and, as Horace knew, a device for introducing into the reader's awareness certain characters who would become crucial later on: the child of the family, William, and the servant Justine, who, through much consideration and care for her education by the Frankensteins, becomes as good as family and socially an equal to them. After Elizabeth's letter and a response from the convalescing doctor, the children read of Frankenstein's rehabilitation at the hands of Henry, and then months go by—almost an entire year. Clerval has been studying Asia—the "orientalists," he calls them—and specifically, Persian and Arabic languages. Horace liked to think that Henry had read Hafiz and Rumi and that he was likewise an "ecstatic" of sorts, a mystic, the perfect foil for his tortured friend.

Victor continued to read of the walks of Frankenstein and Clerval throughout Ingolstadt. The children were elated to learn that Frankenstein was happy again and restored to health. But, as soon as this restoration was complete, they were horrified to read the news coming from home in a letter from his father saying that the young boy, William, Frankenstein's child brother, had been murdered. Frankenstein returned to Geneva immediately. On his journey, passing by what he understood to be the scene of the child's murder, he actually saw the monster in the wilderness and suspected at once that his creature was the perpetrator of the crime. He would find out on returning home, however, that suspicions alighted quickly on Justine, who was found in a delirious state with a locket inset with a picture of Frankenstein's mother—a locket that was around the boy's neck when he was murdered. Frankenstein almost revealed his thoughts, almost insisted he knew who the murderer was, and in fact insisted on Justine's innocence, as did Elizabeth.

And here, before moving on, Victor had to ask, "Is it true, Pinky? Did Great-Granddad kill Frankenstein's baby brother?"

"That's what the good book says, Victor. Although I was closer to it historically, my dealings with Adam were so terribly slight that I have no idea if he would agree or disagree with the details of this story—or, even though he was not good to me, whether or not he was capable of killing a child."

"Grandma says it's true. Mother says it's true."

"I came to *Frankenstein* late, decades after its publication, but your great-granddad would have read it, and I doubt very much your grandmother and your mother would subscribe to its truth without a firm testimonial from Adam. In fact, as you read, I think you will discover, even though the famous doctor paints your great-grandfather as a terrible beast, Mary Shelley, on the other hand, paints him very sympathetically indeed." And Horace knew first hand what it was like killing a child and could understand that there might be a logical reason for doing so—in his case, the protection of another child, and in the case of his father, out of a desire for revenge purer than was conceivable to Horace. He could not, in his wildest moments of anger against Adam, have pictured himself harming his father's children and loved ones; he could not imagine harming a hair on Elizabeth's head. But he also knew that even upon his first moments and hours after his own awakening, he was blessed with an ethical understanding, one that stuck, while Adam—starting from scratch, as it were, in almost every field of human understanding—was more imperfectly formed.

"Why did he do it, Pinky?"

"Keep reading, children. You're doing so well, and it's good to hear the story again. You'll find out everything you need to know. Keep going. You both read beautifully."

It did not take long. Eventually, Officer Babbit appeared on the doorstep, exuberant about Victor's return and anxious to speak to him.

The family stalled on this one as long as it was possible to stall. Mark would say that Victor was not ready to speak yet, or that he was sleeping, or that he was not well and needed his rest. But Babbit kept coming back, and finally they could not in good conscience put the inevitable off any further, despite Elizabeth's objections. Horace kept as still as he could, sitting in the attic in an old rocking chair, falling into a meditative state until the coast was deemed clear for his return to the main floors of the house.

In the living room, with Justine, Mark, and Elizabeth looking on, the conversation between Babbit and Victor went something like this.

"It's good to be back home, isn't it, Victor?"

"Yes, it's very good."

"Where were you all that time, buddy?

"I was lost."

Babbit was making an effort not to condescend. "My! That must have been terrible."

"It was scary."

"You know, the funny thing about that, Victor, is that you must have been *really* lost. We couldn't find you anywhere, and we were looking really hard!"

"Sorry," Victor said.

"Oh, that's okay. You made it home, and that's what counts."

"Okay."

"Did anyone help you, Victor? I mean, did you get home all on your own, or did somebody help you?"

"I found my own way home."

"Funny. A neighbor down the street said they saw someone carrying you."

"Nope."

"Okay. You're the boss. Must have been some other kid being carried down the street. Odd. But that could be. Hey, Victor, I've got one more question for you—and I hope you'll take your time and tell me everything you know. Can you do that?"

"I'll do my best."

"What happened to Jimmy?"

Victor paused for a moment, shocked at the suddenness of it. "Somebody killed him?" he said, tentatively, almost as if it were a question on a quiz.

"Did you see anything? Did you see someone hurting Jimmy?"

"No," he said, and that was the absolute truth. He had passed out after Jimmy struck him. As he was losing consciousness, he remembered falling and then rising again, but he did not say this.

"Do you know who killed Jimmy?"

"I don't know."

"Are you sure about that?"

"I don't know. I mean, yes, I'm sure."

"Okay, Victor. That's probably enough for today, huh? If you think of anything, or remember anything else, anything at all, you let me know. Your folks have my number. Welcome back, there, buddy. It's good to see you safe and sound."

"Thanks, Officer," Victor said.

"But let me tell you one thing, my friend, before I go. People get in big, big trouble for concealing a crime, for keeping what they know a secret. I just want to make sure you understand that." As he said this, he looked over at Justine, Mark, and Elizabeth.

Victor was frightened, and his heart was pounding in his chest. He felt dizzy. "I understand," he said. His parents and his grandmother quickly escorted Officer Babbit to the door, relieved to have him gone, but at the same time ashamed at having to watch the child lie to an adult as they all looked on.

For a monster, Horace's table manners were impeccable. He ate like a gentleman. And he also proved exceptionally helpful in the kitchen, where he did much with Justine to prepare the family meal, which Elizabeth had been attending more frequently than usual. And on the evening of Officer Babbit's visit, having helped Justine with an exceedingly difficult recipe of tandoori chicken, Horace sat at the head of the table, to his right Elizabeth and then Victor, and to his left Justine and Mark. The arrangement was accidental but seemed awkwardly symbolic to Horace, and he secretly hoped no one else was paying attention to it. They likely were not paying attention—or they were and it didn't bother them, seeing as how they sat this way every evening—and when Elizabeth stayed home, her seat remained empty to Horace's immediate right.

The evening was a quiet one at the table, an unspoken fear on everyone's faces as they looked down at their plates.

Elizabeth did finally say, "An excellent tandoori, Justine. Your best, I think."

"Oh, I think Horace deserves the credit here. He's a monstrously good cook."

Everyone laughed.

"I didn't mean that to be funny."

"It's okay, Justine," Horace said. "I thought it was funny. Really. We must be able to laugh at these things—and at these times."

It was quiet again and everyone felt a kind of ease returning to the table, but Victor had been thinking about the afternoon interview and assumed that a terrible secret was being kept from his new monster friend.

"Pinky?"

"Yes, little man."

"Officer Babbit was here."

Everyone looked up at Victor and then turned to see how Horace would respond.

"I know," he said.

"I told him I didn't know who killed Jimmy."

"I understand that. You lied, Victor."

This was a unique moment, as none of the other family members had ever been privy to one of these kinds of exchanges between the monster and the boy. They were momentarily shocked by Horace's didactic tone, but there was something gentle about it, and no one objected.

"It seemed to me that a lie was better than the truth," Victor said.

"Sometimes it appears that way, doesn't it? There are lies we tell to protect people from being hurt, and it's possible that that's a good time to tell a lie. We also tell lies to protect ourselves from hurt or embarrassment, and that's not good. That's cowardly. And when you lie to someone to protect him from knowledge you think might hurt him, that's disrespectful, really, because it is not a decision you have a right to make. It's best, most of the time, to tell the truth instead of a lie."

"The knowledge that you killed Jimmy would not hurt Officer Babbit."

"No, it would please him to know what happened."

"It's kind of sad."

"What's that?"

"That the only person who cares about what happened to Jimmy is this police officer."

"He's doing a job that he cares about, Victor. I don't think he has a lot of love in his heart for Jimmy."

"Probably not. I don't know if Jimmy had any other family or friends. Mother says there was no one at his funeral."

"It's true," Justine said. Had she heard this somewhere or read it? Or had she dreamed it? She couldn't be sure, but she had an elaborate scenario in her imagination, that out of a morbid curiosity, perhaps, she had watched the gravesite service undetected, standing a hundred feet away by another gravesite. A funeral director, a priest, and a gravedigger made short work of the proceedings. And one of them, maybe the gravedigger, made a comment about the tragedy of a child who dies alone, mourned by no one.

And Victor spoke quickly, almost shouting, "Pinky, I don't want you to go to jail."

"That's kind of you."

"Do you want to go to jail?"

"I would like to stay with you and Justine and Mark—and with Elizabeth." He looked directly at her.

"Are you willing to tell a lie to protect your freedom?" Victor said.

"I don't know."

"Are you friends yet?"

"Come again?"

"Have you made friends with Elizabeth?"

"I don't know that either, Victor." He was embarrassed, but he could not help but look at her again. He looked into her eyes, directly.

And she spoke up directly, "Of course we are friends, Victor. How could we not be friends? He has saved your life, precious. And he is kind and gentle and a good friend to this family. And this is the best tandoori I have ever tasted."

After dinner, it was *Frankenstein* night again, and Michelle and Victor held the audience of one very intrigued monster. They were having a discussion about Dr. Frankenstein's deterioration, about his utter despair and sense of culpability resulting from the death of his baby brother and the execution of Justine, family friend and faithful servant, found guilty of murdering the little boy. And they talked about Frankenstein's absolute certainty of the horror that was on the way for him and his loved ones.

"Pinky, it's like what you said at dinner tonight."

"Did I say something?"

"You talked about lies and how people tell them to protect themselves from shame or embarrassment. That's what our doctor is doing." And then, abruptly, he added, "I've done that."

"You have not," said Michelle.

"Yes, I have." For some reason, on this occasion, Victor felt compelled toward a confession. Maybe it was the tortuous situation in which the doctor of the novel found himself and the isolation and guilt that ensued; it scared him, made him feel on the precipice of some giant loss in his own life. And he felt an urgency, some interior warning system that told him that if he did not speak, he would soon be found out.

And a few feet away, where Horace sat in the Morris settee, another realization took hold in the mind of the monster. *My God*, he thought, *Michelle does not know how Jimmy died*. And he made a move at that moment to silence Victor, but he was too late.

"Jimmy's burning accident was my fault," he said.

"Oh, fooey," was Michelle's response.

"It's almost like I killed him twice, because I think that his accident led to his getting into trouble, which led to him killing his papa, which led to him trying to kill me, which led to his death. I should tell Officer Babbit that I killed Jimmy."

"Fooey, indeed!" was Horace's quick and overdone response. No permanent damage had been done yet that could not be got around, and he could tell the information was too much for Michelle to hold all at once.

"What do you mean, Victor, that you caused his accident?" she said.

"I was there."

"You never told me that."

"I was there, and he tried to get me to smoke, and I tried it and choked, and I threw the cigarette at him, and he caught fire."

"You never told me that."

"And I told him to run. He should have stopped and dropped and rolled, but I told him to run. I hated him, and I wanted to hurt him."

By this time Michelle's shock had come into her face, turning it pink with surprise. Her hands shook a little from fear, and her voice trembled. "You never told me any of this."

"I'm sorry, Shelley. I'll turn myself in tomorrow."

"Victor, little man." Pinky's voice was booming. "You must be careful. Yes, if that's true, it was wrong of you to tell Jimmy to run. But too much thinking about what might have been if only you had acted differently—it's not a good thing. I think it might drive you a little batty eventually, thinking that because you stepped out on the sidewalk at any given moment, or that you killed a bug, or that you made a phone call or didn't make a phone call, or that you told a lie, or that you choked on cigarette smoke and somehow caused terrible things to happen later. No, I don't like it." Horace was hoping that the long lecture was preventing Michelle from holding in her memory anything else of what Victor had uttered earlier. "I have had to forgive myself on many counts, to let things in the past stay in the past, and start living in the moment, in the now, and to let other people own their destinies regardless of how I may have helped shape them. Do you know what I mean?"

"No."

"Suffice it to say, Victor, that there will be no more talk of telling Babbit anything. You will remain silent on this. You must carry this on your own with only Shelley and I to help. No more talking. Do you promise? To anyone?"

"I promise," Victor said.

Horace stood up and patted Victor gently on the back and lovingly squeezed his shoulder, and before he left Michelle and Victor alone with Mary Shelley, he said, "Keep reading, kids. You're doing beautifully." He walked out, determined to speak with Elizabeth immediately about this new problem, about this close call, and hopeful that it was not already too late.

It was dark in the back garden, and in this setting, Elizabeth could forget about the homeliness of the man by her side. Listening to his voice, she could imagine his looks in any way that she wanted. She could imagine a Cary Grant, a young Al Pacino, or any number of contemporary and chiseled famous beautiful men. His voice was mellifluous, the voice of a handsome man. It was a shame—a shame that he was not handsome, yes, but also that it mattered. It still mattered. But at the end of all of this pleasant small talk about gardens in the summers of Arizona, about which plants were drought resistant and which ones were not, and about the scents that mingled between the citrus and the floral, he brought up, finally, the question of what should be done about the girl.

"No one explicitly asked Victor to keep this from her," she said. "It would surprise me very much if she does not already know. Shit."

"I don't think she does."

"But what if she does?"

"Frankly, Elizabeth, I trust the girl, but it's a big secret to ask another child to hold on to. I think eventually Victor will tell her if we do not intervene first, and then Michelle might tell someone else—her parents, for example, or Babbit even. God, Babbit may want to talk to Michelle anyway."

"Shit," Elizabeth said. "We should do this. Now."

Michelle and Victor had been sitting alone in silence for quite some time in the study, a phenomenon between the two of them that had become almost a practice. Mostly the silence was relaxed, reverential, almost worshipful, and never awkward, but tonight it was a different color, pregnant as it was with the aftermath of Victor's confession in the mind of the young girl. Michelle could not decide what it was she was feeling. Was it anger at Victor for doing what he had done or for not telling her that he had done it? And was it anger, after all, and not something else—a feeling, perhaps, that she was not in his confidence as much as she thought she was? Was she insulted or just a little bit slighted? And what was that other stuff he was saying? She could not remember it all. She tried to express herself. "Victor, I'm starting to worry."

"About what?"

She avoided the main themes of her thinking by coming back to *Frankenstein,* but this, rather than providing any kind of relief, brought her around to other worries of which she had not even been aware. "Such terrible things are happening in this book—and I'm afraid terrible things might happen to us or to Pinky. You'll break your promise and get into trouble. And I like him and all, but he kind of scares me. And I don't like that you've asked me not to tell my parents about him. This is one of those kinds of lies, I think, that won't do any harm, but sometimes I don't know."

"Shelley, why does he scare you? Is it just because he's ugly?"

"That might be part of it. I don't know if 'scared' is the right word. Freaked out, maybe. But it's not about the way he looks. He's so odd. He's so quiet. He's so smart and old. It's like being in the room with Abraham Lincoln or something—even though it's really cool, it just doesn't seem right, you know, because Abraham Lincoln is supposed to be dead."

"Elizabeth is older than Pinky."

"But she doesn't look like a monster, and she doesn't …"

"So it *is* because he's ugly?"

"No."

"Maybe we could buy him some plastic surgery for Christmas."

"Silly."

"Stranger things have happened."

"No, please, Victor, it's not about the way he looks." She blurted it out. "Sometimes he seems dangerous to me."

"Dangerous?"

She could not explain how when she looked at the monster she sensed a history of unpleasant and frightening stories, of secrets on top of secrets. And maybe it was the way he looked that provided her imagination and her intuition with these clues, but somehow she trusted that if he looked any other way, beautiful or handsome, even, she would feel the same kind of energy lurking under the surface. But then, there was no way to express this. She could not find the words, so she came back to the original theme.

"And I'm worried about you."

"Why?"

"You lied to me."

"No, I didn't."

"Yes, you did. You didn't tell me how you caused Jimmy's burns."

"That's different from a lie."

"No. It's not. It's called withholding information, and it's a kind of lie. I learned that when Daddy had an affair. And what else did you say, that Jimmy tried to murder you?"

"Michelle. Shelley. I'm sorry. Don't be mad at me. Please forgive me. Don't hate me." The tears ran down fast onto the notebook, open to a page where he had written in his notes on the novel, "Why doesn't the doctor tell somebody?"

She could not go on with the interrogation through the tears of her friend. "Oh, Victor, I can't hate you." And perhaps only a second before Elizabeth opened the door to tell her it was time to go home, she had said to Victor, "Don't tell anyone I did this," and she had kissed him on the cheek and tasted the salt of his tears in her mouth.

Of Secrets, Stone, and Mud

After Michelle had left the library, escorted by Elizabeth, an imposing figure appeared at the library door. Horace prevented him from seeing his friend out that evening and immediately wanted an answer to a question. "Does she know, Victor?"

"Does she know what, Pinky?"

"Don't play dumb with me, little man."

"No, she doesn't know."

"*What* doesn't she know?"

"Michelle does not know you killed Jimmy."

"And she must not know. Do you understand?"

"I think so."

"Do you understand?"

"Yes, sir." Victor had never before addressed even his own father as *sir*. But he couldn't leave it completely at this. He felt the need for some further explanation of his dilemma regarding his confidant, the only one he felt he had in the world. "It's hard to keep secrets from the ones that you love."

"Tell me about it," Horace said.

"Well, it's just that—"

"I know what you mean, Victor."

"Then why did you ask me to tell you about it?"

"It's a figure of speech. It's irony. 'Tell me about it.' In other words, you don't need to tell me. I already know all there is to know about the subject."

"I don't like figures of speech."

"Good night, Victor."

"I don't like irony."

"Good night, Victor."

"Good night, Pinky Monster." And he giggled, as if noticing now for the very first time the preposterous nature of Horace's nickname. And Horace laughed too as he left the room, hoping to join Elizabeth one more time that evening in the garden.

Pinky had lived one hundred years with this auspicious nickname. Although he could not remember its exact origin, he knew it came about as he lived with the Mojave people through the end of the nineteenth century and into the twentieth. He arm-wrestled a native and won using only his pinky finger. It was, though, in its general usage, a nickname to signify the monster's superhuman strength, that if he so chose, he could accomplish the most rigorous physical tasks with the least of his appendages. This was also the likely origin of and reason for his acceptance into that culture and his later significant status as a medicine man. He had strength and knowledge beyond the experience of these people, and as he became, in effect, one of the tribe, he also demonstrated profound loyalty and impeccable skill on the battlefield. And Horace lived with the Pinky appellation with a certain amount of pride. He knew what it meant: for one, it was complimentary, and for another, it was infinitely better than the first name the Mojave gave him—Ugly One. Pinky Monster, indeed.

Elizabeth was, as he suspected and hoped, after having dismissed Michelle from the house, sitting in the garden at her favorite spot by the globe mallow. Was she expecting him? He could not know for sure. But he invited himself out, and, walking slowly through the landscape on the gravel path, giving her plentiful opportunities to hear him coming and to request solitude, he approached. And when she said nothing, he sat next to her on the stone bench. "Good evening," he said.

"Does she know?"

“Victor says she does not.”

Elizabeth’s sigh of relief was audible and visible; her entire body relaxed. But there was still some concern. “Do you think he will be able to keep it from her?”

“No. Not for long. Victor is honest and open and wants to confide, and he is a terrible liar. He promised me he would remain silent. It will come down, in the end, between his desire to be open with his friend and his wishes for my well-being and safety. I don’t like the odds.”

“I think the odds are good that he would not want his best friend frightened away by a monster who has killed a child, no matter how terrible the child or how kind the monster.”

Elizabeth was still very much interested in the answer to the query she posed at their first meeting in the garden, and her last utterance brought it back to the forefront and reminded her of the terrible import of what Horace had done. Why had he killed the boy? Had there been no way around it, given the monster’s dexterity and skill? Was she a bit frightened by this man herself? Her formative experience with monsters had thickened her tolerance for the macabre, but years and years—decades and decades, in cold fact—of living without it, except as it would come out in story and lore for the entertainment and edification of a child, had softened her, had made her somewhat squeamish.

“I know what you’re thinking,” Horace said.

“These flowers need dead-heading.”

“That is not what you’re thinking.”

“I wonder if Justine and Mark should replace this gravel path with cement, or stone, maybe. Pavers, perhaps. Do you know, I probably spend more time in this garden than either my daughter or her husband. I think Mark, in his way, was showing his love for me. He built this garden, really. I almost think of it as mine, even though this is not my home. Victor and I have had many conversations here and some difficulties. Once, when his teacher was dying, he came out here and thought he would make her a new pancreas out of stone and mud. He wanted me to bring her back.”

“You could not do that. I mean to say, you would not, even if you could.”

Some words remained unspoken.

Instead, she came to the original thought: "I am thinking that I would still like an answer to my question."

Horace remembered the details vividly. He had been following Victor at a safe distance, out of sight, obscured by whatever became available—a car here, a garage there, shrubbery, and pure stealth. And he had noticed this other kid, too, and was immediately suspicious of his intentions—in part, perhaps, because he appeared to be doing the same thing, tracking Victor. But his demeanor was different and shocking to Horace. He sensed madness and knew Victor was prey. At one point this other kid had taken a detour, and Horace could not follow them both. The boy, through an alternative route, had surpassed Victor and then lay in wait for him, so the attack took both Victor and the monster by surprise. This boy attacked Victor with a kind of demonic ferocity that was familiar to Horace and terrifying. It was the mad passion of hand-to-hand combat, a possession by the singular idea that you must kill and quickly or you will die. But clearly, this kid was in no danger from Victor; he was simply insane with rage. Horace was fast. Jimmy had delivered only one blow before the monster was on him, lifting him into the air, squeezing him hard until the boy's grip on the bat loosened and the thing fell to the grass. And yes, at this point, it would have been physically easy to bodily hold the boy captive until help arrived, but he felt certain this path would foil his intentions. And there was this: Horace, too, was at that moment possessed by something over which he seemed to have no control, an overwhelming rage that took over all of his senses and judgment. The boy's feet touched the ground for a moment. Horace's embrace having crushed the ribs, there was no resistance as the monster's hands grabbed Jimmy the gasoline boy's head on both sides and turned.

"I killed him out of pure, unadulterated passion. I was angry. I could not help myself. I was out of control. I did not really know either boy, but I knew that I loved the one and hated the other. I loved him for what he represented to me. I hated the other because he threatened what the one represented."

"Speak plainly, please."

"I love you still, Elizabeth."

"Shit," she said.

Victor, in his bedroom, trying to get to sleep, was preoccupied by thoughts of Michelle, stinging a bit from their abruptly interrupted evening and the lost opportunity to see her out and say good-bye. But his head was also swimming with pleasure and reeling from that kiss—a token, he imagined, of her unswerving faith in him despite his sins of omission. He decided, then, on one more omission. Come what may, he would keep his promise to Pinky; he could not tell Michelle of the monster's crime against Jimmy the gasoline boy, or, he thought, he would certainly lose her. And it was her judgment and fear, and not the potential danger to Pinky, that frightened him. He could not imagine that Michelle would betray the secret if she knew it. Elizabeth was correct: he made the decision out of fear of losing his friend. Yes, he would keep the information to himself. The only risk he was running was that somehow she would find out on her own. This worried him. Wouldn't it be better, or wouldn't it bode better for the future of their relationship that he be the bearer of bad news? Wouldn't it be better to show her that he trusted she would not abandon him as a result of this information or run to the authorities to report Pinky? Certainly it would be clear that Victor had no part in the monster's decision to end Jimmy's pitiful existence. She would allow him that. Yes, but she would be afraid. But he could assuage her fears; he could comfort her as she had done so many times for him. As he lay there and lay there, it became evident even to Victor that he was trying to talk himself out of the promise he had made. "No," he said out loud to the darkness. "I will not tell her." He tossed and turned, and even when he finally fell asleep, hours later, he was not convinced.

Officer Babbit was knocking on Michelle's family door. Minutes later, a scene not unlike the one at Victor's house days before was taking place in the living room, with Michelle's parents looking on as a friendly officer of the law was interviewing their daughter.

Michelle's parents wanted to be helpful but did not understand how their child would have any new light to shed on the subject of Jimmy's death. She was a friend of Victor's, but Victor, it seemed, was shown to have had nothing to do with Jimmy's sad demise, and certainly Michelle had had no dealings with Jimmy on her own. Nevertheless, Michelle confirmed for Officer Babbit some of the things he'd already concluded: Victor was a nice boy without a violent bone in his body, not someone who was easily angered—not a killer. And Michelle confidently kept within her own knowledge any information about Jimmy's burn accident, and that was not difficult to do, as no one had even come close to connecting Victor with that scene. She did not have to lie, and while she was glad about this, she was nervous still about one important item that finally did come up. The question had already been put a week ago to Michelle's mother and father and had been answered in the negative, but now it was Michelle's turn.

"Michelle, this is very important," Babbit said. "A few people in the neighborhood, on the day Jimmy was killed, reported seeing a strange man walking around and stopping by a couple of public places—a convenience store, a tavern. He is a big man and kind of ugly, sorry to say, according to the reports from some folks. Almost, they say, if you can forgive the language here, retarded looking."

There was an impulse welling up inside of her first to say that Pinky was not at all retarded looking, and no, she would not forgive the language, because she knew exactly whom he was referring to and was deeply offended on the monster's behalf.

"Have you seen anyone like this around your neighborhood? Anyone at all? Even for a fleeting, tiny moment, have you seen any big, ugly, retarded men walking around?"

"Stop saying retarded," she finally said. "No, I have not."

"I'm sorry, little miss, to offend you. This is the word people used."

"Not here, not in this house," she said, "and don't call me 'little miss.'"

And Babbit was impressed by Michelle's sense of propriety but surprised by the violence of her objection. "You have not seen this man?" And at this point, he held up a police composite drawing, terribly inaccurate and almost comical. She could not help but giggle. "No," she said and laughed out loud. "I have never seen that man."

Of Acquaintances and Friendships

The kid Jimmy the gasoline boy had called "Doofus" spent a lot of time that summer riding his bicycle around three blocks of his neighborhood—always the same three blocks. He rode the bike without a thought as to departure or destination, although, eventually, when his legs became sore with fatigue, he would pull back into his driveway, go back into the house, and watch the television alone. The boy had been significantly disturbed by the news of Jimmy's murders, both the murder he committed and his own. He knew that Jimmy was a tough kid—a kid whose prospects were so bleak that he was careless to the extreme in everything he did, finding nothing that posed a moral dilemma for him, willing to do anything for attention or a laugh, most often at the expense and peril of others—but his death was shocking nevertheless. Their friendship was a precarious one, Doofus himself had been Jimmy's victim time after time, but for some reason, he kept coming back to him, kept going to his house, kept up the social connection. Jimmy was, truth to be told, his only society. His own parents were, as far as he could tell, decent enough people, but absent and careless about his upbringing, so much so that they remained ignorant time after time of his truancy from school, rarely kept tabs on his whereabouts, and were ceaselessly lax in all things disciplinarian. They gave him food, a nice place to live, an endless supply of snacks, and the best cable television money could buy, but that was the summation of their contribution to his day-to-day life and the external signifiers of their love for him. He was fat, ugly, and now, extremely lonely. The continuous bicycle loop was about looking for something else to do and someone to do it with and had the added benefit, although this was not foremost on his mind, of providing something called "exercise" that was most of the time foreign to him. The loop of three blocks happened to include Victor's street, and one very lucky day on a fine summer morning, Doofus saw Victor in front of his house retrieving the mail.

"Hey, Frankenfucker," he shouted, almost cheerfully.

Victor turned around to look and saw the fat boy across the street riding his bike rather unstably down the sidewalk. He recognized him but could not immediately place him.

"Terrible about Jimmy," the boy added, and then Victor remembered.

Victor did not respond verbally to either greeting, but watched carefully, hoping the boy would simply continue down the road, dreading any further conversation or connection. He had begun deliberately down the pathway to his front door when he noticed that the boy was crossing the street with his bike and coming toward Victor's house. He heard him shout "Hey" before Victor closed the door, pretending to be oblivious to the fat kid's further attention. Relieved, and inside, leaning against the front door, he breathed deeply against his racing heart. Beginning to relax, pulse returning to normal, in the next second Victor found himself jumping out of his skin with the knocking on the door, three loud raps followed by the chiming of the doorbell. Victor considered hiding in his room. Justine and Mark were at work, and Pinky would not answer the door. The fat boy would go away. But Victor's sense of decorum was overpowering, and he turned around and opened the door to face this sorry visitor.

"Hey," the boy started right away, "I'm sorry I called you Frankenfucker. I didn't mean any harm. It just came out, you know, because I was so used to hearing Jimmy say it. I didn't mean any harm. Victor, I know your name is Victor, and I won't call you Frankenfucker or Franken-anything, for that matter, for as long as I live, cross my heart and hope to die right here this very minute."

"What's your name?" Victor said.

"Doofus."

"That is not your name."

"Unfortunately, yes, it is actually my name. It is, however, my last name. Reginald is my first name. I don't like that name, though. You can call me Reggie or you can call me Doofus, but don't call me Reginald. Is it a bargain?"

"Sure."

"I was just out exercising." He patted his round belly. "I was out on my bike when I saw you getting your mail, and I didn't know you lived here, and it's been such a long time since I've talked to any kids, so I thought I'd say hello and formally introduce myself. My name is Reginald 'Reggie' Doofus. Howdy, neighbor."

"Hey."

"Can I come in and meet the folks?"

"No," Victor said, too vehemently, perhaps. "I mean, my parents aren't here, and I'm not supposed to have anybody over."

"You don't have a sitter or nothing?"

"No, I'm by myself."

"That's pretty cool. Me too. I'm what they call a latch-hook kid."

"Latchkey."

"Latchkey, whatever, some kind of latch. That's me. It means my parents are never home. But they don't care one way or another if I have friends over. I don't often have friends over, though. I don't know why. I guess I just don't think of it. I'm kind of a solitary individual, a loner, I guess. But I had Jimmy over once, and he almost burned the house down. I miss him. But he was a fucker."

Victor stepped out onto the front stoop and closed the door behind him. This boy, this Reggie kid, was going to prove difficult to shake, Victor thought, and so rather than take the chance that Pinky would show up in the background of the house, Victor decided to continue this interview out of doors.

"My God," said Reggie, "did you hear what happened to him? Somebody just broke his neck and left him to rot on the ground. Officer Babbit's been poking around looking for the monster who done it. But maybe he had it coming, I suppose. Did you hear what he did to his own daddy? Shit, I would never do that to my dad. He'd kill me. You know, maybe Jimmy was, in fact, killed by the ghost of his daddy. That'd be something."

"Do you believe in ghosts?" Victor did not really care for an answer.

"Yeah, sure, why not?"

There was an awkward silence, here. Victor was sizing up the kid, trying not to be obvious, looking away when Reggie looked him in the face, looking at his face when Reggie looked away. He was fat, but on closer inspection, he was not that ugly. Victor realized that obesity was connected in people's minds with unattractiveness, unfairly, perhaps. Some of his family members were no strangers to this phenomenon; although none of them were fat, they had other physical eccentricities competing with the aesthetic appeal of their faces. This boy was not that ugly after all. And his loquaciousness, while a bit of a challenge for Victor, was in some way endearing.

"Hey, if you don't mind me asking—but if you do mind me asking, just tell me, and I'll shut up—but if you don't mind me asking, what's up with all this Frankenstein stuff? I mean, why did Jimmy and those other kids do that? Are you a Frankenstein nut or something? A super fan?"

This kid, because of his irregular school attendance, thankfully, did not know the story, had not been there in the first grade when Victor made the claim that would cement for his classmates forever his reputation as the crazy kid who thought he was a relative of the famous monster. "So tell me, don't be shy now, are you a super-duper fan?"

"Yeah, I guess so," Victor said.

"That's all right. I can get behind that. I don't know nothing about Frankenstein, but I do know a lot about other things. I know a lot about *World of Warcraft*, and I know a lot about superheroes and comics and things. Hey, is there someone in your house?"

"No."

"Well, shit. I thought I saw somebody in that window there."

"No. Nobody is home."

"Well, I better get going. Gotta keep up my routine, you know. I think I've lost a couple of pounds. Anyway, maybe we could be friends or something. You know, I'm not like Jimmy. I don't even know why I hung around him. I'm sorry he was such an ass to you. I'm not going to make you smoke or call you names or any of that. My God, that was something else, that one time with the cigarette and the fire. I thought he was a goner then. And you told him to run! Dummy. Everybody knows you're supposed to drop and stop or something. Roll, yeah, that's it. You're supposed to roll. Everybody knows that. Anyway, I live on Lambert Street. You can come by anytime, and we'll watch TV or play games or something. Do you have a bike? We could bike."

"Yeah, I've got a bike."

"Maybe we could bike, then. Hey, I'll see you later, Victor. You're all right." And with that, he remounted his bicycle and pedaled away.

"Who was that?" Pinky said once Victor was back inside.

"That was Doofus."

"It's not nice to call people names, Victor."

"That's his name."

"Sure it is."

"Pinky, were you just walking around in the front room? I think Doofus saw you walking around in the front room. The curtains aren't all the way closed."

"That was not I. The boy Doofus is seeing things."

And whether Reggie Doofus was seeing things or not, Victor was terribly uncomfortable with this new acquaintance even thinking he saw someone in his house that was not one of his parents and at the prospect of a new friend, especially one who could connect Victor to Jimmy in any other way. Reggie presented an unpredictable variable that Victor felt he might have to control. He was not sure which path would present the most danger, leaving him alone or befriending him. He might, out of necessity, have to associate with this boy, but it would have to be on his terms and away from Victor's home and Pinky's hiding place. That was likely not a sustainable strategy.

Victor decided to leave the boy Reginald Doofus alone. But two days later, Reggie was knocking on the door, this time in the evening when Mark and Justine were home. He introduced himself to them, made them laugh, and asked if Victor could come outside to play. Victor feigned illness, and that worked two evenings in a row. But on Reggie's third visit, Victor felt he could no longer maintain the ruse and agreed to go outside and at least visit for a while, Reggie's charm having won over his parents to the degree that they scolded him for shunning this new potential friend and almost insisted that Victor entertain him. It seemed Victor had no way out of the association after all.

"So, you been sick? I was sick once with some god-awful thing. I thought I was gonna die. I was even in the hospital for a time. Mumps or the croupa or pox or something. Wanna go for a bike ride? I've been exercising every day. I think I've lost a couple of pounds. Do I look thinner? Do you think I look thinner?"

Victor could see no appreciable change in the boy's girth. "Yeah, I think so. A little bit, maybe."

"Do you want to go for a bike ride?"

"Not really."

"Hey, are you still hanging out with that girl? Jimmy said you had a girlfriend. I think I saw her once last year on one of the few days I was actually at school. She was pretty. Jimmy was jealous. What was her name? You still going out with her?"

"We're not going out. We're just friends."

"Oh, yeah, I know how that is. You don't want to get too serious, you know. After all, you're only in the fifth grade."

"Right."

Reggie was assessing the situation. Victor stood there, unenthusiastically, waiting for something to give. "Well, what do you want to do, then? You wanna come to my place and watch the tube? Play a game? If you don't want to bike, what do you want to do? Are you still feeling kind of sick? I know that time I was sick, it took me a week to feel like doing anything, even after I was well. I was all weak and stuff."

There was Victor's escape route; he had known that if he waited long enough, Reggie would provide one. It was something that Victor noticed, a skill that unpopular kids developed of providing excuses for other people not to spend time with them. "Yeah, I'm still not feeling all that well. I should probably go back inside."

"Well, suit yourself. I don't want to prolong your illness, you know. I'm going to go home and microwave something for dinner. Hey, look. Speak of the devil. Your girl."

Up the street and toward the two boys pedaled Michelle on her bicycle. Entering the summer preceding her fifth grade year, her parents allowed her more autonomy to go freely about on two wheels. They no longer drove her around the neighborhood.

This evening was not a *Frankenstein* night; Victor was not expecting her to visit. His surprise and delight at seeing her was palpable to Reggie. He could see Victor beaming. "Just friends," he mumbled. "I can see you're starting to feel better already."

Michelle approached and stopped the bike, and her hello to Victor was accompanied with the kind of smile Reggie had never seen on a fifth grade girl. His experience of fifth grade girls was extremely limited, but he knew that there was a quality in her manner that was more adult than childlike, a maturity that made him immediately uncomfortable. He excused himself and prepared to pedal home.

"You don't have to go," Michelle said.

"Oh, you know, Mom and Dad will have dinner ready, and I should get back. Family time, you know. See you, Victor," he said as he pedaled away. Michelle and Victor watched him disappear in silence. They stood there together, and finally, when they could no longer see Reggie's bicycle, Michelle, without looking at him, almost accidentally, reached out and grabbed Victor's hand. They did not look at each other, but both were smiling blissfully as they looked down Victor's street at nothing.

"Who was that boy?"

"I'm sorry I didn't introduce you. I'm kind of sorry. He's odd. He wants to be my friend, but he talks too much and he skips school all the time."

"And he's fat?"

"No, that has nothing to do with it. He's exercising. He's trying to lose weight."

"What's his name?"

"Reginald Doofus."

He waited but was shocked and immensely impressed when Shelley did not laugh at the boy's name.

"Reggie was a witness to Jimmy's burning," Victor said.

"Oh."

"We can't let him know about Pinky."

"I know."

"Pinky killed Jimmy to save me."

"I know."

"I'm sorry I didn't tell you."

"I know. I love you, Victor."

Nights before, Victor having gone out for dinner with his parents, Michelle had paid Pinky and Elizabeth a visit. It was a bold move for one so young, but Michelle, as we have seen, brought other qualities to bear that most children her age would take years to develop, if they ever developed them at all. Michelle had caught on to a degree of secrecy around her and between Victor and these family elders that had made her uncomfortable and suspicious. And knowing intuitively that it was these elders, and not Victor, who were responsible for it, and knowing also that Victor was out of the house and Pinky and Elizabeth were in, she cycled over and confronted the monster and Victor's grandmother. She learned the truth about Pinky's responsibility for Jimmy's death, which she had suspected on her own very early on, and she took it with an amount of stoicism and seriousness that impressed these very aged individuals—so much so that they ceased to worry about her either purposefully or accidentally revealing this information to anyone who might use it against them. She had already passed her muster with Officer Babbit, and there would be no other occasion for him to confront her.

While things in their immediate circle seemed as tight as they could possibly be, Pinky was anxious and tired of hiding. He had spoken to Elizabeth about going far away, leaving his family with relatively uncomplicated lives. But Elizabeth knew that he would not, could not leave yet. And Pinky knew it, too. He was testing the waters. He was desperate to determine if there was any reason for him to hope that Elizabeth would return his love and worried, too, about something that Victor had said at the very close of his captivity, something that Elizabeth had said nothing about, something of which she had shown absolutely no sign. Elizabeth was dying, Victor had said. *But aren't we all*, thought the monster, *to some degree or another?*

Of Losing Parts

It had come to pass that Adam died in a very strange way, in the same way, Elizabeth thought, that her brothers would have died had they not been killed in a war, and in the same way her sisters-in-law would have died had they not killed themselves. In some respects, losing life on the battlefield or through suicidal poisoning while in the comfort of your own bed seemed more attractive than the way her father died—and the way she feared she would go, too, unless there was some kind of intervention. Was it a condition unique to monsters or one summarily passed on to any monster offspring? She could have no idea. But the truth remained: Adam lost his parts, one at a time. It was as if his body was in total mutiny against his longevity. And there was no rhyme or reason to it, there was no logical sequence. First he lost complete use of the right arm at the elbow. It became a frozen limb at the end of which only the fingers operated. The left foot followed, requiring him to rely exclusively on crutches for locomotion. Then the left leg failed him, and next came the humiliation of dependence on a walker. Fingers, one at a time, on the left hand and then the right, alternatively, went numb and became useless stumps. An ear, only one, lost its receptiveness to sound. Adam felt, early on and as he started to suspect some kind of progression, that he was being erased from the Earth. But then—and maybe this was a saving grace—after the initial nightmare realization but before everything was lost, his mind started to go, so that, in the end, when there was not enough of him to sustain any kind of life, he had no idea what was happening. He was giggling like an idiot.

And all of this was in the forefront of Elizabeth's thinking now because she started to notice that her body was in rebellion. The impulse would begin in the brain, but the message did not always arrive. *I'm going to walk over there,* she would say, and sometimes she would walk, and sometimes, inexplicably, she could not move—or she would not move. There was no struggle to get the legs to propel her, no physical stress, the kind of which you see when a limb is being asked to do something it's unprepared to do. None of that. Just nothing. A desire to walk followed by no walking.

And this was the first evidence that caught Horace's attention. She had said she was going in to get a glass of wine. And she just sat there. Or she had said that she wanted to pull that particular weed, and then, uncharacteristically, she remained immobile and simply stared in the direction of the offending plant. Or she had said, "I'm taking off this sweater," and nothing followed. It was strange to see someone who was so decisive become such a procrastinator, or to become forgetful like this, or to say things she wanted to do that secretly she wanted other people to do for her. Horace could not figure it through, and so he asked, on a particularly warm evening when Elizabeth expressed the desire to jettison the extra garment and then was frozen, whether she needed help with the sweater.

"Are you kidding?" she said.

"No, not at all. I just wondered if you wanted some help with the sweater."

"Are you getting fresh with me?"

"Well, then, take it off. Make yourself comfortable."

"I'll take it off when I'm damn well ready to, thank you."

"You said you were too warm, maybe a half an hour ago. It's just an observation. I'm going to bed." He stood up and walked toward the house.

"Me too," Elizabeth said, and she remained stock still on the bench.

But as Horace lay in bed, drifting in and out of sleep, he believed he knew what the problem was. It was not at all about being a monster or about being in the hereditary line of monsters. It was simply this: despite her still youthful appearance, Elizabeth was old. Through the ages, it was true of both monsters and men. Old age was a killer.

And one day Elizabeth woke up in darkness. She could not see, and it was terrifying. She could barely dress herself. She could not see to prepare food; she could not see to drive; she could not see to dial the phone. She fumbled her way through her house and stumbled carefully over to the neighbor's for help. Afraid of ambulances and hospitals and doctors in general, she insisted her neighbors call Justine and Mark first, and that is what they did. Independence was now officially and probably permanently gone. Even though she felt like she lived there already, she now knew that she would have to move in permanently with Mark and Justine, the only benefit to which, she thought, was to never be too far away from Victor—or, she had to admit, from the monster.

Victor was happy that Grandma Elizabeth was with them now, too, but he was terribly frightened by her new condition. It was painful to see her become dependent on others—not that he understood that part of it, but he could tell how angry it made her, and how sad, that Justine and Mark were always there to help her with the simplest, most mundane things. And the notion of permanent darkness was especially horrific to Victor. But he noticed that when in his company, or in Pinky's, Grandma's vitality returned. She was energetic and lively, only blind. Because he suspected that Elizabeth's time with him was in short supply, and wanting to take every remaining opportunity to be with her, Victor spent an inordinate amount of his time with Elizabeth and Pinky in the library, reading together, listening to stories about the monster family, hearing about this monster's adventures with the natives of Arizona, and learning something singular, but for Victor inexpressible, about old age—its richness, its breadth, and its tenacious potential. Something new was happening between Pinky and his grandmother; he could feel it. And he knew it with certainty one evening, when they asked him if he would leave them alone for a while so that they could have a little monster talk.

"Your grandmother and I would like to do some necking," the monster said.

"Yuck," Victor said as he slipped quietly out, giggling and inexplicably happy.

"Horace," Elizabeth said.

"Call me Pinky."

"No. That is a childish nick name and I want to call you Horace."

"It is not childish. But all right, then, call me Horace."

"Thank you. I will."

The second hand on the grandfather clock made its circuit five full times before the next word was spoken as they sat together on the Morris settee.

"Horace. I want you to kiss me."

The monster had absolutely no problem with this request. There was no hesitation, no second guessing, just an immediate response to the invitation, an invitation he thought might never come, an invitation that made his monster heart beat like a gigantic concert bass drum. Elizabeth knew what was coming, had predicted accurately this result and the quality of its execution. Somehow she had known he would be an excellent kisser. She was blind, and she felt like she had just been kissed by a god. "That settles it, then," she said.

"I guess it does. Can you love me only now that you can't see me?"

"Yes, I can. Now I can."

"It doesn't matter to me."

"I knew it wouldn't. Do you think I'm foolish?"

"No. I love you, Elizabeth. Let's go away. I have a place, a cabin in the desert—a place we can live together in peace. "

"I'm dying."

"No, you're not."

"Yes. Don't argue."

"Okay."

"I'm not ready now. But when I'm ready, I will know it, and I want you to do something for me."

"Okay."

"I want you to help me die before I lose my mind. Can you do that, my love, my monster love?"

"Yes. I can do that, Elizabeth. Trust me."

"I do trust you, Horace. I do."

Elizabeth closed her eyes, fell into the monster's arms, nestled her head against his great chest, and fell asleep. His tears fell down his face in great streams, into her hair, onto her forehead, eventually blending with Elizabeth's own tears into one continuous river.

Of Third Wheels and Another Reunion

Having been displaced, at least for this evening, by Pinky helping Elizabeth convalesce in the family library, Victor and Michelle sat outside on a bench in the garden. Victor was annoyed by his neighbor's cigarette smoke. He found it ironic that since smoking had become illegal in almost every indoor public establishment that the only place any more where you had to deal with this kind of pollution was outdoors. He was beginning to appreciate irony. And there was some, Michelle and Victor had found, in the chapter of *Frankenstein* in which the doctor is confronted for the first time by his monster. The monster tells his story to his creator in the most eloquent language, in perfect King's English—no grunting, no moaning, no roaring at torches, only Mary Shelley's perfect prose bringing to life the voice of the original monster, Adam, bringing to the doctor's imperfect understanding Victor's great-granddad's experiences in the forests and villages around Ingolstadt.

"Can you smell that smoke?" Victor was terribly distracted.

"No, not really. Concentrate, Victor. This is important."

"I know. I know."

And then, suddenly, there was an interruption and further distraction from Justine. "Victor, Shelley, there is someone here to visit. Here they are, hun." And to both of their surprise and to Victor's unspeakable dread, Reggie appeared and was directed into the garden where they sat with their sacred text. "Hey, what's going on?" he said. "What are you playing?"

"We are reading, Reggie."

"Whatcha reading?"

"You would not be interested." Victor could not withhold his perturbation, and even against his better judgment, he knew he was being very unpleasant.

The invitation came from Michelle. "You are welcome to join us, Reggie."

At first he was excited, honored to be allowed into this circle of association, to be able finally to approach the mystery of Victor's Frankenstein stuff. But given a turn to read out loud, he was embarrassed by his lack of fluency, and then, as a listener to Michelle's proficient song, he was further embarrassed that even while the material was read expertly, he could not follow the sophistication of the sentence structure or the advanced vocabulary of the monster. "This sucks," he ended up saying.

Michelle was patient, overmuch so, Victor thought. She skillfully guided Reggie through some difficult passages, as Mrs. Terhart used to do, Victor remembered, and this made him love Shelley even more deeply. But his love for her was tinged with something else, too, an emotion that was new to Victor, although he thought he could name it. It was unpleasant and uncomfortable, and it was aimed squarely at Reggie. He was jealous of Michelle's attentions, and though he understood that it was irrational, could not shake it, just as he had found it nearly impossible to shake this new friend. Victor became even more incensed as he watched Reggie's eyes start to brighten, probably at a new understanding—but it looked suspiciously to Victor like something else, admiration maybe, or the beginning of an infatuation, perhaps, or even love. This thought was more than Victor could stomach, and he found his attention waning and his fingers and feet tapping until finally, he heard himself say, "It's getting late, and that smoke is driving me crazy. Maybe we should call it quits for the night." It was the only time he had ever thought of cutting short his time with Michelle, but desperate times required desperate measures.

"We're just getting started, here, Victor," Michelle said.

"Yeah, we're just getting started," Reggie said with new enthusiasm.

"Maybe I'm not feeling well," Victor said, lamely.

Michelle saw right through him. She knew what was happening, and even though she was momentarily flattered, she didn't like it. But she knew it would be unwise to confront Victor now, unwise to bring this new acquaintance into any kind of confrontation or to embarrass anyone by the suggestion that, at least in somebody's mind, there was some kind of competition going on.

"Well, maybe"—Reggie thought he was being accommodating—"you could go inside, and we'll continue the monster's story. We'll catch you up later."

Victor wanted to attack him.

"No, Reggie," Michelle said, and Victor's heart immediately lifted from its deep chasm. "Victor and I have a little arrangement. We don't read ahead. We have to stay together."

"I see. Oh well, that's okay. I'll go home then. But you give me a shout when you're going to continue, because I'd really like to check this out some more. I mean, I could never do this alone, you know. It's kind of hard and stuff. But it seems like a good story. It's a lot different than that old black and white film with what's-his-face, Karamazov."

"Karloff," Victor said, contemptuously. "Boris Karloff."

"Yeah, that guy, Karishnokov. Well, I'll be seeing you then, Victor and Michelle. Thanks for letting me read with y'all." And with those words, he left the backyard through the side gate and was gone.

Some silence passed, then, between the two children. Victor broke it by saying what he thought was obvious, true, and real. "We can't spend a bunch of time with this kid. He can't know about Pinky. He can't be over here all the time—especially now that Grandma is so ill and Pinky is with her and not in his room at night."

"Victor, you're jealous. You're not worried about Pinky. You're jealous."

At first, it was Victor's impulse to defend himself angrily, to shout down the charge, but with one look at her smiling in a perfectly knowing and accepting way while her eyes revealed not a little bit of devious pleasure, Victor was disarmed, and he laughed. "He's such a—I don't know what. A doofus."

"He's sweet, Victor. And harmless. And could use some help with his reading. Don't worry. He's not going to become a project of mine."

Victor ran a little fantasy through his mind in which Michelle created a kind of reading monster in Reggie. He would be transformed. He would become brilliant. And he would lose weight and become attractive. It was a funny thought experiment, but he didn't like that last part and quickly revised it so that Reggie would remain perpetually fat and at least kind of ugly. He laughed out loud.

"What?" she asked.

"Nothing."

Michelle was not conscious of anything deliberate on her part, but it did come to pass that Reginald Doofus was in fact a regular attendee at weekly *Frankenstein* night get-togethers, and that he did in fact become a kind of project, but it was a project of his own design, not hers. He insisted himself into this role and endeavored to become a reading monster. Somehow he knew that in the end, the only thing that might distinguish him from a no-good scoundrel like Jimmy the gasoline boy was his level of literacy, a literacy that he was getting neither in school nor from his family and just barely from his television. Somehow he understood that knowledge was power, and this was something for which he had a little more than a fleeting interest.

Time passed, as it will do, and fifth grade was in full swing. The math was more complicated, the geography of the planet was made explicit, there was less time to play, the teachers were more serious-minded and less lovable, the reading load was elevated, and the vocabulary more intense (but not especially difficult for fourth graders who had been reading Mary Shelly). Reginald Doofus had become more than adequately equipped with these latter skills and had been attending school religiously, and, perhaps as a result of that constant circling around the block on his bicycle, which had become less aimless over time and more intentional, he had lost weight. Victor was furious with him. Michelle, as benevolent as ever, kindly urged Victor to get over himself, reassured him that there was not a chance on the planet that her feelings for him could ever be displaced by this new friend of theirs, and would assuage the fear altogether, at least temporarily, by planting a chaste little kiss on his cheek.

And something else very strange had happened in Victor's social circle that also helped relieve the feeling of competition with Reggie. There was a new student in the class, and the moment this boy walked into Mrs. Carter's fifth grade classroom, Victor immediately felt a shock of recognition that practically took the top of his head off. In fact, on seeing the boy, Victor let out a cry of excitement against his will and found himself, as the boy hung his coat up in the closet, rushing over to embrace the kid. It was Dennis. No doubt about it, it was Dennis. It was an awkward moment for which Dennis was not prepared. Much had changed, and two years for a grade schooler is a long time—enough time for some kind of tragedy to callous over the soft spots of childhood, for early cynicism to creep in—so at first, Dennis did not know who was hugging him and worried that he was in the wrong classroom, a classroom full of idiot children. But then, when Victor stood away finally and Dennis had a chance to look into his face, he recognized him and perhaps forgot momentarily about his third grade kindness. "Frankenfucker," he said.

For a moment Victor thought he had made a terrible mistake. "Dennis?"

"Yeah, it's me, all right. I'm back." And then Victor could see that the boy was doing some internal work, processing memories and experiences, adding things up, and then realizing his error. "Oh, Victor, I'm sorry I called you that. Forgive me."

This was his Dennis, after all. What other fifth grader, besides Shelley, perhaps, would say to another fifth grader, "forgive me"? But Dennis was not a fifth grader, Victor remembered. "Shouldn't you be in the sixth grade?" Victor said.

"It's a long story. I will tell you about it," he said, but it was time for both of them to come back into the classroom proper, settle down at their desks, and begin the day's first lesson, a little piece about American history and the signing of the Declaration of Independence.

And on one evening, only a few days after Dennis's return, Victor made a decision that would have been inconceivable to his imagination only a week before. It was a *Frankenstein* night, one of the very last, as the three children had reached the penultimate chapter in the novel, and Victor had asked Michelle and Reggie to postpone the reading. And when the suggestion was not well received, he agreed to let Reggie and Michelle go on without him, and he agreed also that he would read the chapter for that night on his own. Victor had made plans to have Dennis over, and that night, unfortunately, was the only night in the week that was good for Dennis. The excitement about catching up with this long-lost friend completely overshadowed any thoughts Victor may have had about Reggie with his girl, alone—or, more significantly, perhaps, about breaking the long-standing tradition and ritual of reading *Frankenstein* with Michelle.

So, two parallel scenes were unfolding simultaneously in different houses in the same neighborhood on the same evening, and at least two of the parties involved, one at Reggie's house, the other at his own house, were singularly conscious of something slightly askew: the world not quite spinning at the correct axis, the stars not sufficiently aligned, and an indescribable and tentative danger in the air—so tentative that it was pushed away in the minds of the two parties, suppressed, dismissed, and finally forgotten. And it was raining. It was raining in Arizona, a hard, summer monsoon rain.

"What is this?" Dennis said.

"I think it's raining," Victor answered, listening to the pounding on the rooftop from inside the library. Victor and Dennis were sitting at the table at which the reading was traditionally done, a closed copy of the *Frankenstein* novel resting on the corner under the reading lamp. Why they had decided to sit there was unclear. Victor had introduced his parents to his returning friend and had been giving Dennis a tour of his home, a kind of whirlwind tour, a tour that included only a cursory look into the floor where the bedrooms were and where one of the rooms, Pinky's, was decidedly closed to inspection, and they had stopped here in the library at the very end and settled down to chat over a couple of Dr Peppers and a bag of chips.

"No, what's this book?"

"Aw. That's *Frankenstein*."

"I can read, silly," Dennis said. "You're still into this stuff?"

"Well, yeah. I started reading it a long time ago, and I'm almost done. It's not an easy book to read, and we've been reading it out loud, Shelley and I, which slows us down, and we've been reading it with this other kid, too, and that slows us down further."

"I thought you had already read it."

"In the second grade? Are you kidding? No, I knew the story, but I would not have been able to read that book then. Too hard."

There was a moment or two when neither boy spoke, and while Dennis looked away in a kind of awkward silence, Victor looked directly at his friend's face, thinking to himself about whether this was, in fact, that same boy. He came to the conclusion rather quickly that yes, it was, and the face, while it had changed some, was familiar again and brought back into Victor's emotional landscape all of the feelings he had once had for Dennis. And in a moment, Victor was overcome with joy and gladness at his friend's return. "I thought you moved away because of me."

"That's silly."

"Why'd you come back?"

"My mother is dead. I'm living with my father now. My mother and I moved to California and she became very sick, and when she was hospitalized, my grandmother took care of me, and I missed so much school that year it put me behind. And then when Mom died, my dad asked me to move back here with him."

"What did she die from?"

"It was cancer."

"Mrs. Terhart died from cancer."

"She was a beautiful woman. That's sad."

"Well, I'm sorry about your mom."

"Yeah, it was terrible. You know, my parents got divorced a long time ago. The worst part, I think, the worst part for me, was that Dad was not there when she died. Mom didn't seem to care about that, though. How do people do that? They just forget. They go away from each other, and then it's almost as if the other person never existed. Dad came up for the funeral, and that's when we made the decision to live together again."

"Do you like your Dad?"

"Oh yeah. I missed him terribly. And he missed me. You know, adults are just stupid. No, that's not it. It's that they get stuck—in their jobs and in their homes. Dad could not come to California to follow Mom in her new work. He was stuck. And Mom had to go—she had to work, and until she found work, she had to live with her family. *She* was stuck. It seems adults sometimes don't have any choices. We talked almost every day on the phone, Dad and I, and I know he was very sad that we were apart. And I was sad."

"I can't imagine," Victor said. He was thinking about the separation between creators and monsters, fathers and sons, about ultimate separations. "I did not forget you, Dennis."

"That's nice. You're not like most people, Victor. I don't want you to be mad, but I almost forgot about you. I mean, for awhile I thought a lot about those times talking on the playground and about that night you came over and how you scared the living daylights out of Mom, and I was sad we didn't have a chance to say good-bye or even for me to tell you where I was going and why I had to leave. But, you know, years go by. New town, new school, new friends—everything crowds in. I almost forgot about you. Don't be mad."

"I'm not mad. Sometimes I have difficulty remembering Mrs. Terhart. I have to work hard to think about her, to picture her. I understand."

"It all came back at once after you hugged me. That was kind of embarrassing, Victor. Kind of dumb. You don't want kids calling you Frankenfag again."

"I don't care," Victor said. "I don't care," he said again. "There's a bright side, you know, to forgetting. Kids have forgotten. They don't harass me any more. If I get grief from other kids now, it's usually about being smart, even though I'm not smart, I just work hard, or sometimes I'm teased for having a girlfriend, but not anymore about being related to monsters."

"So, you're still saying that—or, I mean, you still believe it."

Victor was taken aback. Suddenly he realized how much indeed his friend had changed over time. He felt betrayed. "*You* believed me, Dennis."

"Yeah, Victor. I was in the third grade."

Of Reading Alone with the Third Wheel

Reggie lived in a nice house, Michelle concluded, albeit cold. There were nice things everywhere, but something was lacking. Well, warmth was lacking. There were no books. There were high-quality furnishings and a beautifully appointed kitchen and an elaborate and clearly expensive entertainment set-up, but there was a sense that these things were not really enjoyed or appreciated by anyone—except for the entertainment center, of which Reggie was clearly proud. It was the first thing he showed her, even before introducing his parents, who were in a spotless kitchen (they had eaten out) drinking martinis together. In fact, even though the two children had a clear purpose here tonight, that of reading the twenty-third chapter of *Frankenstein*, Reggie was compelled by the television, asked Michelle if she wanted to watch a show or to play *World of Warcraft* on the computer, and then, further distracted by his most recently acquired hi-tech toy, wanted to show her a game he could play on his new cell phone.

"No, Reggie, we're here to read."

Reggie's parents were dumbfounded.

"Where do we go, Reggie?" And Reggie, slightly disappointed but successfully shrugging it off, led her into a living room area out of sight of his parents, still sitting awestruck in the kitchen. Again, it was a finely appointed room that appeared meticulously maintained but completely disused. Comfortable, but no sign of life. They settled on the couch together, a respectable distance between them, Reggie still fiddling with his phone. Michelle opened her copy of *Frankenstein* to the twenty-third chapter and told Reggie to turn off and put away his toy. And when he complied, and as the rain poured down on the rooftop of the Doofus household, she began to read out loud.

After the most dramatic turnaround, after the monster's story is told, after the refusal to make the monster a bride, after the swearing of eternal battle between the monster and his creator, after another murder of vengeance, and after the last in a series of fatal abdications of paternal responsibility, the doctor married his childhood companion. He took her to an inn at a lake by a town called Villa Lavenza. It was a beautiful place in the Alps, but the weather was stormy—the wind and rain were violent that night.

"That's funny," Reggie said as Michelle finished reading the first two paragraphs of the chapter. "It's nasty outside here, too." He was only slightly aware of making some kind of profound realization: sometimes, what happens in books is echoed in the world of the reader.

"Reggie," Michelle said, calmly but with a seriousness that hinted at her slight misgiving about the likely success of this reading session without Victor. "I need you to let me read for awhile without interruption. We can talk when we get to something good."

"Okay, yeah, yeah, yeah, you're right," he said.

The doctor was fearful, and his bride was nervous. He told her that everything would be fine if they could make it through that dreadful evening, and of course, he wasn't talking about the weather, but thinking about the last words his monster had spoken to him. A promise was made; the creature swore that he would be with Frankenstein on his wedding night.

Michelle and Reggie both were engrossed by the story, but perhaps not as fully as they could have been or would have hoped to be. Michelle had serious doubts about the wisdom of reading this climactic chapter without Victor and felt a little guilty of something, not because she was alone with Reggie, but because she realized that her decision to move on in the novel without her best friend was a kind of punishment for Victor, one that she was not fully conscious of when the decision was made. So the whole time she read, she was longing to be able to share it with Victor, and she was imagining the kind of wonder and enthusiasm with which he would have greeted the words on the page and the way the reading would continue, as it always did when they read alone, to deepen their childlike but evolving intimacy. She became a bit overwhelmed by these distractions, and so she asked Reggie to take a turn reading out loud.

Reggie had made such dramatic improvements over the several months he had spent sharing in this endeavor that he could read with almost perfect fluency now, getting stuck from time to time on the more difficult vocabulary, like *physiognomy* or *incredulity*, and still failing to read with exactly the proper emotional tone or register. Nevertheless, it was satisfying to hear him read, and Michelle could not help but smile with pleasure at his miraculous trajectory.

Reggie was reading of the doctor's despondency as he returned to his hometown after his final, greatest loss and defeat: the death of his bride. The doctor studied the environment he remembered from happier days, but everything was now a shade of gray—everything was dark. He had lost all hope, and he wept. Reggie noticed Michelle smiling as he read out loud: "Nothing is so painful to the human mind as a great and sudden change." He stopped reading and sat in silence, looking directly and intently at Michelle.

"What's wrong? Why did you stop?" she said.

"I was thinking about this."

"What?"

"This sentence. It just sort of stopped me. Sometimes the opposite thing is true, I think."

"I don't know what you mean."

"I want to thank you, Shelley."

"For what?"

"Shit, for *what*? Are you kidding? For teaching me to read. For changing my whole deal. *'A great and sudden change.'* Although, I'm not in pain like the great doctor—I'm happier than I've ever been in my whole life. I'm a different person now, and it's all thanks to you, Shelley."

"Please don't call me that."

"Why not?"

"It's not my name."

"*He* calls you that."

"It's different."

"Well, you know, I like Victor and all that, but the fact of the matter is, he's got a new friend, a friend that he's with right now, a friend that he chose to be with tonight rather than be with you. What do you think about them apples?"

"Reggie, they were best friends, and they haven't seen each other in a long time. It doesn't mean anything else." And now that she was saying it, she believed it, and she felt guilty for the thoughts she had earlier—thoughts that Reggie was articulating in this distasteful way.

"Well, you can believe that if you want. I don't."

"Shut up and read, Reggie."

He had no choice but to obey. He continued to read. The doctor failed to engage the law in an effort to track down and punish the monster, became enraged at the inefficacy of the powers that be, and concluded that another route must be found to realize this mad ambition to destroy his creation. And as Reggie continued, something welled up inside of him not entirely unlike what Frankenstein was feeling—an anger at others who refused to see the truth, a kind of desperation to help them come to their senses, a realization that if you want something done the right way, you might have to do it yourself. But unlike the doctor, who had lost everything he loved, Reggie was feeling the possibility that he might rather gain something he had never had. He could taste it. He didn't want to let go. "I love you, Shelley."

"No, you don't."

"Well, yes, I most certainly do."

"This is all wrong, terribly wrong. It was a mistake to come here."

"And I am going to tell the world. And I'll start by telling Victor. I'm going there right now. You coming?"

And before Michelle could say a word to stop him, Reggie was out the door without a coat into the rain, and she followed close behind, hearing the ineffectual voice of his mother calling from the kitchen, "Where are you going there, honey?" as Michelle closed the door behind her.

Of Rituals to Read to One Another

"So *what* you were in the third grade!" Victor was still beside himself with the thought that his truest childhood friend and confidant had somehow chalked up his acceptance of Victor's family history to childish naïveté and gullibility.

"I'm sorry, Victor. I'm surprised. I thought you would have grown out of it, too. I didn't mean to offend."

"Offend? It's as if you've put a stake through my heart."

"No."

"Yes, Dennis. A family history is not something you grow out of!"

"Well, unless it's a fantasy."

"You believe that? That I made it all up?"

"Not exactly. Well, yes, in fact, I do."

"There's someone I want you to meet, Dennis."

This was an unprecedented move for Victor, and he felt it in his bones. But he also felt it was a safe risk to take, so sure he was of Dennis' goodness, so sure he was that Dennis was a boy that could be trusted, and so strong he was in his need for vindication. "You wait here a moment, Dennis. Don't move. Just wait."

"Whatever you say, Frankenbuddy."

His plea to Pinky was desperate. And Elizabeth was there, acknowledging him but not seeing him. Victor's parents had gone out, so Pinky and Elizabeth were together in the living room, and Victor approached them with the request that Horace reveal himself to a stranger—a request he made with a kind of violence or passion that they had never seen Victor exhibit, except perhaps in his effort to save Mrs. Terhart. He was adamant. He was almost shouting. And when he was finished with his plea, there were some moments when nobody spoke and the only audible sound was the continuous rain on the rooftop and Victor's quiet sobbing. The monster spoke. "Why is it so important to *prove* what you say to your friend? Isn't trust the true test of friendship, and wouldn't it be a surer sign of this boy's loyalty to you as a friend if he would just take you at your word?"

Victor knew it was true. There was nothing else to say on the matter. Without saying a word in response, he returned despondently to his friend in the library.

"What is it?" Dennis said. "Who is it you wanted me to meet?"

"My monster great-uncle. His name is Horace, but I call him Pinky. And he's alive, and he's living with us."

"Well, where is he?"

"He won't come."

"Oh. I see."

"His life is in danger if he's discovered here."

"Oh. I get it."

"You don't believe me."

"Victor, it's good to see you again, and I hope we can be friends. But I'm just not sure, you know. It seems crazy to me." Dennis was thinking and wanted to articulate that Victor, in every other way, seemed like a normal kid, like the kid he remembered liking so much a couple of years ago—but that a normal second grader talks of monsters in the family, while fifth graders tend to jetison these fantasies. But he couldn't find the words, and he stumbled over the ones he could. "I can't be sure of anything. You know, shitty things happen." His parents' divorce, his mother's death, local and international convulsions of which he was constantly but vaguely aware—all these things weighed on him. "It makes me not want to believe in things, especially things like this. I believe things when I see them. I'm like that guy in the Bible."

"Doubting Thomas?"

"Yeah, him."

"Horace, my monster uncle, whom I call Pinky, says that a true friend will take you at your word."

"But Victor," he said, and again tried unsuccessfully to find the right words. His experience was that people he loved and people who loved him lied to his face. His mother had told him her illness wasn't serious. His father said he knew nothing about it. His mother said she wasn't cheating on his dad. In a false macho pose, his dad told him he didn't love Dennis's mother, never had. All lies. Dennis found that he couldn't even take *his parents* at their word, and not because they were bad people, but because they were wrong, they made mistakes, and they were afraid. "I'm not saying I think you're lying to me. Maybe it's just that you won't let go of the idea."

Victor was crying. Dennis was sorry. He put his hand on Victor's shoulder and it felt awkward, so he took it back. Instead, he scooted his chair closer to Victor's chair, reached his arm all the way around both of his friend's shoulders, and embraced him. He held him while he cried, and then there was a sound. It was the sound of the library door opening, and Dennis suspected it would be one of Victor's parents. He thought momentarily about releasing Victor, but then he thought better of it and left his arm around his weeping friend. He looked up to greet the visitor, and he saw an old woman standing in front of him. Because she was not looking at him, not even remotely, he judged she was blind. She left the library door ajar, and spoke. "Victor? Is everything all right?"

"Yes, Grandma Elizabeth. Come in."

She felt her way into this familiar place and found a seat on the Morris settee behind the two boys. "Introduce me to your friend, Victor."

"Grandma Elizabeth, Dennis. Dennis, Grandma Elizabeth."

"I wonder, if you boys aren't doing anything, if you would do me a favor."

"Sure," said Dennis, and this was a surprise to Victor.

"I have trouble sleeping unless I read for a while. Now that I can't read and I haven't had the time or inclination to pick up braille, I've got to have somebody read to me. Would you boys be willing to do that? Would you read to me?"

"Sure thing." It was Dennis again.

"Why don't you read from where you left off in *Frankenstein*, Victor?"

Victor grabbed the book from the corner of the reading table, turned on the reading lamp, and started in with chapter twenty-three of Mary Shelley's novel.

And while Dennis had never read the book, he had no trouble understanding what was happening here. He could put two and two together to figure out that the narrator of this passage was the doctor on his honeymoon, that the enemy he spoke of was the monster, and that by the end of this short passage, the doctor was reduced to emotional rubble and was desperate for revenge against the murderer of his bride. And the reading, expertly delivered, he thought, by his friend Victor, nevertheless did little to revive his faith in Victor's story, but rather exacerbated his doubt, for who would want to claim this monster, this murdering fiend, as a great-granddad? Only a delusional child would do that. But there came into Dennis's awareness another presence in the room. Even before he turned to look behind him at Victor's grandmother, he knew there would be someone else sitting beside her. Victor felt it too. This guest had entered soundlessly during the reading and was in effect invisible until the very end of the chapter. Victor turned happily around to greet him, and Dennis turned around in terror. Victor put his hand over Dennis's hand and said, very softly, "It's okay. Don't be afraid."

And the monster said, "Let's finish this book together, shall we? Read to us, Dennis, if you would be so kind." Then Dennis, loathe to contradict this request from such a singular personage, began to read, faltering at first through nervousness and fear, and then finding confidence as he realized with every moment that passed in which nothing terrible happened that he was beyond safe and was, in fact, being held like a fragile thing in the most caring of hands.

Reginald Doofus and Michelle entered the room as chapter twenty-four was already in progress, but Michelle begged and pleaded as she hugged Victor like she hadn't seen him in years that Dennis start over from the beginning so that she and Reggie would not have to miss anything. Simultaneously, the wind was taken completely out of Reggie's sails, not only when he saw the embrace between Michelle and Victor, but especially when he saw the creature sitting next to the old woman on the settee. Michelle's intense affection toward Victor put a temporary pall over his plans to usurp the young lovers, and as the sight of Horace, a bona fide monster, indeed, filled him with awe and morbid curiosity, he subsequently forgot what he was about. He was sopping wet. The monster told him to take off his wet shirt and brought him a blanket from a chest of drawers in the corner. As soon as he was dry and warm, he seated himself across the reading table from Victor and Dennis, Michelle sat herself down between Horace and Elizabeth on the settee, and Dennis started again at the beginning of twenty-four, over the noise of the rain, pounding more violently than ever over the rooftop of Victor's home. "My present situation was one in which all voluntary thought was swallowed up and lost," he read.

Justine and Mark understood too late what was happening. There was no time to prevent Elizabeth and Horace from introducing the family secret to two strangers, two more children in the circle. And after returning home from dinner, when it finally dawned on them that grandmother and the monster were alone in the library with these four kids, they were frantic with anxiety, both of them pacing in the kitchen and in the living room and wherever else pacing was possible. Justine would let fly a "Jesus H. Christ" every half a dozen paces, and Mark grumbled under his breath, without irony, about Elizabeth and her blindness.

"This will not do," Mark said.

"There's nothing to be done about it now," said Justine. "We'll just have to cross our fingers. Jesus."

"We should not have let him stay here. Aiding and abetting, I think they call it."

"Again, Mark, there's nothing to be done. Coulda, shoulda, woulda."

"This may ruin us."

"No, they'd have to prove we knew something. Wouldn't they?"

"I'm not a lawyer. I count beans. This is out of my ken."

"Mark, we should calm down. It may come to nothing. Or, as Elizabeth likes to say, something good may …"

"Blah, blah, blah," said Mark, and the conversation was over.

The doctor stood in the graveyard over the tombs of his young brother, William, his wife, Elizabeth, and his father, swore the oath toward absolute revenge, and prayed this unholy prayer: "I call on you, spirits of the dead; and on you, wandering ministers of vengeance, to aid and conduct me in my work. Let the cursed and hellish monster drink deep of agony, let him feel the despair that now torments me." Reggie felt the anger again, the anger of the doctor toward the monster, the likeness of which was now in the room with him, not four feet away, and strange things started to happen in Reginald Doofus's brain. He started to identify with the doctor's rage, but simultaneously to transfer this feeling toward the real monster in the room. And then he began to imagine Victor, his new friend Victor, whose girl had taught Reggie to read and to live, also as a kind of monster, somehow in allegiance with the one Dennis was reading about, and with this other one, there on the settee, sitting next to Victor's girl, who, by rights, he thought, should've been his. He had not acquired all of this new skill and awareness for nothing.

The doctor hunted his creature all over creation and was goaded all along by the monster, who, just as Frankenstein faltered from weakness and fatigue and hunger, left food to sustain him and messages to provoke him—taunts scribbled in dirt or inscribed in stone. "My courage and perseverance were invigorated by these scoffing words; I resolved not to fail in my purpose." *Here is a man*, Reggie thought to himself, trying not to let his attention stray too far from the words being read from the page, *who is absolutely dedicated to his cause, who will stop at nothing to get what is justly his.* I *could do that. That could be* me. Perhaps he understood, but perhaps not, that the monster in this history was similarly imbued with a sense of mission and destiny: to drain every ounce of spirit and hope from his master before Frankenstein's life came to a miserable end in the torturous conditions of this frozen landscape. Certainly, coming to the end of the tale, Reggie had great difficulty discerning in this story who was the hero and who was the villain.

He began to concentrate his gaze on the monster sitting in the room with him, apparently focused deeply and reverently on the words read out loud by Dennis, his eyes closed almost as if he was asleep. And suddenly, from the recesses of Doofus's uncharted mind came an imagined scenario that was intensely compelling. It was just a hunch, but it acted on his spirit with the certitude of natural fact. *This monster here, the one they call Pinky, this gentle giant sitting across from me listening with closed eyes—this creature must have killed Jimmy the gasoline boy.* For what reason or in what circumstance, Reggie could not imagine, but now he was almost sure of it. Maybe it was that Jimmy sought revenge against Victor for his burns, and maybe it was that this monster preempted Jimmy's attack. That seemed very likely. "The spirits of the dead hovered around, and instigated me to toil and revenge," said Doctor Frankenstein, and in that moment Reggie felt as if the spirit of Jimmy was likewise hovering, trying to tell him something, urging him toward this conclusion. He started fingering the cell phone in his pocket. One trip to the bathroom and a phone call, and it could be over. He would be a hero. Dennis was reading some of the last words the great doctor would speak to his confessor, his nurse, the explorer whose letters bookended Mary Shelley's masterpiece: "Swear to me, Walton, that he shall not escape; that you will seek him, and satisfy my vengeance in his death … if the ministers of vengeance should conduct him to you, swear that he shall not live—swear that he shall not triumph over my accumulated woes, and survive to add to the list of his dark crimes." And through the last fifteen pages of the novel, while the three other children, one blind old lady, and a monster were riveted by each word, this boy, still fumbling with the cell phone in his pocket, lost all his powers of concentration on the novel. Reginald Doofus did not understand the ending.

Of an Early End to the Fifth Grade

There had to be a celebration at the conclusion of this great endeavor, the accomplishment of such a heady task for fifth graders: the successful reading of Mary Shelley's *Frankenstein*. And it had to be done in-house, because it was of great moment to the children that Pinky and Elizabeth be present for the revelry, and it had to involve all four children, much to the chagrin of Mark and Justine. Conversely, though, it would afford Victor's parents a closer look at the two new children they were dealing with—an opportunity to size up the danger. A party was set for one week after the reading of the last page. Mark and Justine could not know, however, that the opportunity to size up these kids would come sooner than they expected.

In the days that followed that last reading, some singular developments occurred. One was that Dennis, so impressed as he was with his experience of Pinky, coupled with his appreciation for the ending of a novel, the rest of which he had not read, took some solitary time over the next few days to read Mary Shelley's novel from the beginning. Meanwhile, conversations between the children about the end of the novel revealed that Reggie's understanding was less than perfect. It was as if, Michelle thought out loud one afternoon and Victor concurred, that he had checked out for the entire last few scenes. And additionally, Reggie had been behaving strangely, avoiding Michelle and Victor together, but deliberately seeking them out when they were alone and striking up awkward conversations morbidly focused on the more gruesome details of the *Frankenstein* story: those of grave-robbing, surgical reconstruction, and the murder of children and innocents. His intentions were clear enough to Michelle: it was obvious that he was trying to shed light on the gory details in hopes of dissuading her from her attachment to Victor and his family. But Victor was as yet ignorant of Reggie's confession of adoration toward Michelle, and Michelle, for her part, had decided to keep mum. Why embarrass the boy? It was harmless, after all, and Reggie would recover. Victor, however, chalked his strange encounters with Reggie over the next few days up to the boy's inherent eccentricities. Then, on the day immediately preceding the *Frankenstein* celebration, the following conversation took place, after which Victor found himself in a serious dilemma.

Out of the blue, and as plain as the light of day, Reginald Doofus announced to Victor on a walk home from the bus stop, "I wish Shelley did not love you."

Victor was astounded by the brazen nature of this announcement, and deeply offended at his flagrant and unearned use of a pet name that only he and Grandma Elizabeth had used, one that had become sacred to him. "Take that back, you—" Victor searched for the worst thing to say and was unsuccessful. "That's a mean thing to say."

"Someday soon she will love me instead, and she will think your family is insane, and that you're insane, and that your monster great-uncle is a criminal."

Suddenly, those last few words made Victor tremble; he shook with both anger and fear. "You don't know what you're talking about."

"Oh, yes, I do, homeboy. You can't pretend any longer. You can't hold the secret any longer. You know what I'm talking about, don't you?"

"What the hell *are* you talking about?"

"Jimmy, Victor, remember Jimmy? What happened to Jimmy? Do you know? Do you know what happened to your good buddy Jimmy? Remember that day you almost killed him by setting him on fire and telling him to run like a chicken without a head? Do you remember that, Victor?"

"What of it?"

"Well, I think Jimmy came to see you about that after he recovered from his burns, had a score to settle perhaps, was going to do you some serious harm, but someone helped you. Someone came to your rescue. Who was that, Victor?"

"I should have known better than to befriend you, you piece of shit."

"Wow. I have not heard expletives like this since—geez, I don't know, since Jimmy was alive. He was a first-rate curser. You got some work to do, but it's not bad."

"What do you want, Doofus?"

"I'm so glad you asked. I was thinking you'd never ask. I don't have squat in this world. I'm all set for cable, but I don't have any people in my life that matter, and my parents wouldn't know the difference if I were dead. But now I can read, and I think I can think, and it's all because of Shelley. I want Shelley. You tell her to buzz off. That's what I want. And I'll keep your secret."

"Are you insane? Even if I did what you ask of me, she could not love you, not for a moment."

"Oh, but she could, and I think she will. I could win her. And if I couldn't win her with my smarts and my charm, my smarts and my charm could trick her well enough into choosing me. You want to protect your monster. She'll want to protect your sorry ass. She will be with me, one way or the other."

"You can't force people to love you, Doofus. It will never work in the long run. It will end in your misery, that's for sure. But you know, I'm not even going to consider what you're saying to me. We're done, Reggie. I don't ever want to see you again. I don't want you coming to our *Frankenstein* party. I don't want you a mile from my house or the people I love. We're done. Good-bye and good luck." And at that moment Victor sped up his walk to a jog and gained on Reggie a considerable distance until he was able to walk home alone in tears of fury.

Sobbing, Victor stood before his family. "I don't know how he knows, but he does!"

"How could he possibly know, Victor?" This was the voice of Mark, beside himself with frustration, not wanting to blame his son but unable to avoid voicing the implication.

"I swear I did not tell him. Even Dennis, who I love, I have not told."

"We believe you, Victor," Elizabeth said, and his mother nodded in agreement.

"I think he just made it up, just thought it up," Victor said, "and he's convinced he's right, and it turns out that he *is* right."

"Okay, what do we do now?" Mark, again, wanted a decision to be reached in the quickest possible way.

"I can leave here," Horace said and was immediately surrounded by tearful embraces from Elizabeth and Victor.

"It would probably be the best thing," Mark said.

"For whom?" Elizabeth shouted down her son-in-law in the dark.

"For us, Elizabeth. This is, after all, our home and the neighborhood in which we must live."

"You *must* live nowhere."

"What are you saying, Elizabeth—that we pack up the whole family and run away? Are you kidding?"

"You would not understand, Mark. You married into this, and you have never embraced it or understood it fully."

"Thank you for that vote of confidence, Elizabeth."

"I will go," the monster said again.

"No, you will not!" Elizabeth shouted.

"I will stay, then, and go to jail."

Elizabeth caressed his face and could feel the tears streaming down from his eyes, and she held him tight. "Take me with you," she said. "You can go if you take me with you."

A certain relief came over Mark, and a dread came over Justine and over little Victor—a feeling of complete abandonment. "No," Victor said.

A decision was reached, by whom and how it was not clear, but Victor remembered his grandmother saying, "We're having the party now. Call Michelle. Call Dennis. We will have one hell of a *Frankenstein* party, and tomorrow we will be gone, Reginald Doofus and Officer Babbit be damned. Do it, Victor. Call them."

Michelle was easy to convince, fully aware as she was of the seriousness of the problem, and Dennis, while not at all privy to the reason for this haste, trusted Victor implicitly and made quick arrangements with his dad to get there for the celebration. It was very much like a literary-themed birthday party. There was no time for any kind of elaborate decorations, but there was the constant buzz of book group talk while the children ate cake and ice cream and the adults drank scotch and looked on—or, in Elizabeth's case, listened, and held on to Horace's arm. All were amazed but depressed. The children were happy, but Victor and Michelle were somewhat subdued, and this, coupled with the mysterious circumstances of the hasty date change, gave Dennis the feeling of being slightly left out of the loop. A voice inside his head told him to trust his friends and that if there was something new to know, he would know it soon.

Among the topics for discussion was the question of why Walton gave up the mission when the ice broke free and, against Frankenstein's advice, turned back home for London. Then there was the question, too, again flying against Frankenstein's wishes: why didn't he act against the monster when he showed up on the vessel? They were all struck, too, by the monster's last words, the pitiable desire to expiate himself to his dead creator, yes, but also his sheer despondency and his ultimate wish to end his life. What must have happened inside Adam's mind, as he left that ship and disappeared on the horizon, in order to totally transform his purpose from death to life, we can only guess at, as we have done already at the very start of this narrative. But the children wondered at these things, as each of them privately wondered at their present circumstances and thought hard together in silence until one of them spoke.

Dennis said, "It's too bad Reggie could not be here."

And by now, for Victor, lying had become out of the question where friends and family were concerned. "Well, Dennis, it's because of him that we changed this date. He has become strange and dangerous to my family, particularly to Pinky, and we cannot have him here. And Pinky must leave our house and go far away, or we fear that Reggie will expose him."

"Has Pinky done something wrong?"

Victor was lost in thought. It was a superb question. Had Pinky done something wrong? He could confidently answer in both the positive and the negative, and it gave him some considerable trouble to realize that the jury was still out for him. Victor started to speak, but Dennis held up his hand to stop him as much as to say he didn't want to know. Victor got the message and was silent and in awe of his friend, and Dennis followed up with this statement, perhaps intended as a kind of ruse for the adults, who noticed the children whispering: "It's too bad Reggie couldn't be here."

Earlier in the evening, when those phone calls from Victor must have taken place, Reginald Doofus, unsatisfied with Victor's last words to him and loathe to give up so easily, had set up a vigil outside Michelle's home, saw her through the window on the telephone, and watched as she left the house, opened the shed, retrieved her bicycle, and rode away. Yes, he followed her to Victor's, and throughout the passage of time during the *Frankenstein* celebration, he was waiting outside the house—for what, he was not sure. But he had done a lot of thinking and had come around to the conclusion that Pinky was not, in fact, the monster he was looking for. Yes, there was the Jimmy question, and ethically, someone should be held responsible for the murder of even the most reprehensible human being—but ethics were not foremost on Reggie's mind. He could not fool himself anymore with this conclusion. No, his love for Shelley was foremost on his mind, a love of monstrous proportions, a monster love that compelled him to do what he barely was conscious of doing, like this waiting outside of Victor's home for some supernatural miracle that might unite him with his paramour or bring him face to face with the enemy. No, he knew that Pinky's fate was only a bargaining chip, one that proved futile in moving aside the obstacles in the way of Michelle returning his steadfast dedication and love. Yes, the only real obstacles were Michelle's feelings for Victor and, of course, Victor himself. Take care of both of these problems, or even just one of them, and success is assured. Michelle was proving a hard nut to crack, as dedicated to Victor as Victor was to his monster great-uncle. That left only one other option. His anger seethed through every joint in his body.

He continued to wait—for how long, he had lost complete track. He only knew that his legs were growing tired of this stationary position, outside Victor's home standing in between two cars parked in the driveway, his right hand sweaty and his fingers cramped, gripped as they were in a tight fist, his nails digging into his palm. The pain grew unbearable. At first, he did not know where it originated, coupled as it was with a different kind of pain, the one in his chest pounding his heart like a hammer. Finally making a distinction, he unclenched and opened his fist and saw his hand, bathed in the floodlight above the garage door, bleeding. Then, something miraculous occurred within his teeming brain, and he began to see. As he looked at his bloody hand, he started weeping, and through the tears he was able to see. He saw what he had become after a few short months of simply reorganizing the patterns of his life. He saw Jimmy the gasoline boy, dead, unmourned, unloved forever. He saw Victor, who had taken him in despite his annoying gibbering, and Michelle, who, like the friend or the teacher of whom he had never thought himself worthy, had encouraged him, coached him, believed in him, did not love him but cared for him deeply nonetheless. He stood there, paralyzed and weeping.

The party was over, it appeared. As the front door opened, Reggie ducked down, and Dennis emerged, giving cheerful good-byes to his friends still inside. Reggie remained crouched between the two parked cars. Dennis walked down the length of the driveway on the opposite side, came all the way down to the sidewalk, and, almost directly behind the silent Reggie now, pulled a cell phone out of his jacket. He was phoning his dad to inform him that he was on his way home, walking. When Dennis, still talking on the phone, had moved down the sidewalk a couple of houses, Reggie stood up and walked toward Victor's front door.

Reggie knew it was unlikely they would let him in. If he knocked now, immediately after Dennis's departure, they would think it was Dennis returning for some forgotten item or to say some forgotten thing. They would open the door, and Reggie would have an opportunity, a single opportunity, he thought.

Dennis was still on the phone four doors down having a very unusual conversation with his otherwise easy-going father about how Dennis should move quickly and talk to no one, that he'd be meeting him in the car, and that, in fact, he was already en route. Dennis was flabbergasted but understood from his father in relatively short order that a man suspected of murdering a child, a large, ugly, slightly deformed individual, was perhaps on the loose in the neighborhood. His father had learned from a new friend, who happened to be the detective on the job, that the culprit was likely close by.

Dennis moved quickly toward home. He was afraid, but not for himself. He had said nothing to his father, but he was convinced that the suspect in question was not roaming the neighborhood at all but was sitting in Victor's house on the Morris settee, and that his friends were in grave danger. Yes, Pinky had done something wrong. Suddenly, he felt strangely vindicated, somehow, and also foolish that he did not see it—he had been hoodwinked just like Victor. Poor Victor had imagined that his ugly and deformed great-uncle was part of some literary myth come to life, a lie his whole family had perpetuated and inflicted on Victor since he was an infant. This Pinky was, after all, a monster, to be sure, and he had polluted his friend's childhood with a fairy tale to cover up his malevolence. Momentarily, a vision of doing the heroic thing to save his friends overwhelmed him, and without waiting for his father, who was, no doubt, only blocks away in the car, he called 911 on his cell phone and reported the fugitive's whereabouts.

Victor had opened the door and was so astonished to see Reggie there in tears that he could not obey his first impulse to slam the door in his face. He could not even ask what he wanted before Reggie had spoken through sobs of regret. "I'm so sorry, Victor. Please forgive me. Please let me come in. I'm so sorry." Immediately, Victor was disarmed and allowed his new friend to enter. There was such good feeling in the home at the conclusion of this most auspicious celebration that no moments were wasted in this reconciliation. After receiving some first aid to the injuries on the palm of his right hand, Reggie assured Victor he would not be making any moves on his girl, and he assured Michelle that he would say no more about it and that he understood how completely in fifth grade love she was with Victor. He told them how thankful he was to both of them for taking him into their society, teaching him how to read and become a human being, and introducing him to the family history and this wonderful, beautiful, miraculous monster named Pinky.

And at that moment, Officer Babbit arrived, as if he'd teleported. He had been patrolling in the neighborhood when the 911 call came, having felt in his bones that he was finally on to something significant, and filled with the adrenaline of hot pursuit and the likelihood of a dangerous engagement, he had left his vehicle in flight almost before it had come to a complete stop. And when he busted through the family door with the certainty and authority of justice personified, he saw the monster holding a boy named Reginald Doofus aloft in a celebratory embrace and thought for sure the boy was in grave danger. And even while Justine and Mark and Michelle and Victor all yelled at him to stop his pursuit, Babbit mistook their tears of joy for cries of peril. His weapon was out, and he was shouting at the monster to put the boy down. Horace, in a panic, carrying the joyful but confused Reggie in his arms, burst through the back door of the house. Elizabeth, terrified by what she could not see, cried out in darkness. Horace let Reginald Doofus drop into the backyard. Babbit saw the boy flounder on the dirt, bewilderingly, yelling at *him*, as if *he* were the bad guy. Horace ran, Victor emerged from the house and chased him, and a gun was fired. No matter that Horace should have been an easy target; the shock of seeing him and the backward nature of almost every minute detail of the situation must have terribly shaken this veteran officer. He missed the monster clean, and Victor lay face down in the back garden.

Epilogue: Of the Children of Monsters

Victor was just a boy, but the macabre elements of the family history had made him aware of a certain number of myths or stories that surround the experience of dying. For example, he had heard about how life flashes before the eyes, he had heard about light at the end of a tunnel, and he had heard stories of voices speaking out, sometimes calling forward, sometimes urging return. How much of this was true for Victor? The bullet killed him instantly, so there was not a long and drawn-out process of letting go. There was an instantaneous firing of the brain before it became quiet and still, and in that firing of the final synapses, a few of these stories, with some exceptions, became a part of Victor's dying. A light, yes, appeared at the end of a tunnel of darkness. He moved toward it eagerly, as it appeared comforting and warm rather than bright and harsh. There was a whispering as he moved that seemed to swirl around his head. The first distinguishable words were Mary Shelley's: "My imagination, unbidden, possessed and guided me." And then there were voices from his life. There was Mrs. Terhart, comforting him, telling him he was a favorite, urging him to ignore the taunts of his classmates. He heard Jimmy the gasoline boy laughing. He heard Dennis's voice that first day on the second grade playground: "They're just jealous that they don't have monsters in their families. Would you like to be my friend?" Then it was Jimmy's voice again, trying to insult him with new variations of Frankenstein but unable to complete a single slur. Doofus was telling him that he loved his girl but knew her heart belonged to Victor. Grandma Elizabeth was saying that something good would come from this. Justine was urging him not to be too truthful. The last voice he heard was the voice of his great-grandfather, Adam: "Light, feeling, and sense will pass away; and in this condition must I find my happiness. Some years ago, when the images which this world affords first opened upon me, when I felt the cheering warmth of summer and heard the rustling of the leaves and the warbling of the birds, and these were all to me, I should have wept to die; now it is my only consolation." Then, finally, as Victor grew closer to the light, he felt soft kisses on his cheek and forehead, unmistakably from the lips of his dearest friend in life, Michelle. He couldn't see her. He struggled to see her, felt himself turning his body this way and that to get a glimpse, desperately searching. There was nothing but darkness all around and the light ahead, and he kept moving forward, and he thought he was crying. Into the light, he moved.

Babbit was out cold in the back garden. It had happened so fast, and nothing in his experience could have prepared him or protected him. The gun had been fired, the boy was down, and before he could blink, it seemed, the monster was on him and the blow came and he was knocked over like a sack of potatoes. Justine and Mark were baffled. They had watched the ordeal unfold in a kind of stupor, and now, as they stood in their garden with an unconscious officer and two children in shock, overwhelmed, and mute, they tried to make sense of it. Horace was gone. Elizabeth was gone. And they had taken their boy, their beloved Victor, without an explanation, without a word. The parents had been unable even to assess their baby's condition. They saw him fall after the shot but were not sure if he had been hit, had tripped and fallen, or was diving for cover. He didn't move, there on the ground, but that could have been fear, or he could have been unconscious. Mark thought he saw blood, and when he said this, Justine crumpled into a fetal position and wept on a small plot of grass. "Where's my baby?" she cried.

In Elizabeth's car, Horace drove faster than it was safe to drive, miraculously without notice or incident, away from the suburb, away from the city, and into the vast desert countryside. Elizabeth sat silently in the passenger seat in pure darkness, in terror, and in grief, for miles, until she had to know what the driver of this runaway vehicle was thinking and what he planned to do with the precious cargo she knew they were carrying. The dead child lay as if asleep across the back seat of the Subaru. "Where are we going, Horace?"

"We have some work to do, you and I."

It was some time after Horace's oblique response to her query before finally Elizabeth understood what her monster lover had in mind. There was no more conversation in the car until their arrival. The agreement was tacit and complete.

What seemed to Elizabeth to be hours later, they arrived at the cabin—the cabin that Horace had procured years before, the cabin built by Elizabeth's brother William, the cabin to which the monster had secreted Victor some months before, the cabin to which he had hoped he and Elizabeth could escape under very different circumstances. Now it was to be set up and made ready for this most auspicious and sacred job: the job of bringing Victor back to life. He was clinically dead. It was their only chance at restoring the universe to its proper condition.

Adam had made significant improvements and advancements to Dr. Frankenstein's original work, and then, shortly after he created his last monster and before he lost the hope and will to live, in one last creative outpouring, immense leaps forward were made, theoretically, over his own art. These secrets were passed on. Elizabeth knew them and had intended to apply them to June Terhart; Horace had learned them but had never had an appropriate opportunity to use them: ways of preventing the brain from dying, ways of kickstarting the heart, ways of making the blood pump again, ways of reanimating dead tissue and organs, and clean, less horrific ways of replacing and rebuilding appendages if necessary—methods that would perplex and astound any twenty-first century physician.

Close at hand, everything they needed was there—all the necessities for the work and any and all creature comforts they could possibly desire to make this passage safe and pleasant, if not absolutely joyful. In a few short days, all their preparations were accomplished, and arrangements were made with a local medicine man for transport and delivery. The work was made short and effective, and afterward, Horace and Elizabeth had some time to spend with this new monster before sending him home and fulfilling their final responsibility on the earth.

"Welcome back, Victor."

"I feel funny," were the first words in his new life.

"Do you know us?"

"Yes."

"What do you remember?" asked Pinky.

"Tell us everything you know," Elizabeth pleaded, caressing his cheeks, kissing him, and weeping in her darkness with joy.

Victor spoke his monster talk. Haltingly at first, and then more fluently as the places and people of his last life came flooding back into his revitalized brain—a staccato list of wonders. "My name is Victor," he said. "I hear bells. They're starting to go away. I cried a lot. I feel better. I remember things. Classrooms. Graham crackers and milk. The smell of crayons. I remember the playground. Asphalt. Grass. Swings and jungle gyms. Sawdust. The bench I sat on. There was a breeze blowing through the leaves on the trees, and I met Dennis one day, and he made me feel like a normal kid. Meanness is no great thing. Kindness is stronger. Mrs. Terhart was my fourth grade teacher, and I tried to build her a pancreas but couldn't. She died. There are things we can't change. Jimmy smelled like gasoline and burned. There are people nobody loves. There are stories within stories. I read Walton's letter to his sister, and within those letters I read Dr. Frankenstein's story, and within the doctor's story I read letters from Elizabeth and his father, and within the doctor's story I heard the story of great-granddad, Adam, the first monster, and within Adam's story I heard the story of De Lacey and his family, the beautiful Arabian and her evil father. Father. Family. Some people are in the dark, in blindness, about the necessity of father and family. You are Horace, my great-uncle Pinky, the monster that saved my life by killing a child. And you are Elizabeth, my grandmother, my sweet, dear grandmother who taught me everything

I know, nearly, next to Mrs. Terhart, who died because I could not make her a pancreas. Mary Shelley. Mary Shelley wrote our book. I know her. Shelley. Michelle. Shelley. We read together. She kissed me once. She is a perfect person. There is no such thing as a perfect person, but she smells like home and loves me. Oh God. She thinks I'm dead. My love thinks I'm dead."

Victor wept. Pinky and Elizabeth made no overt effort to comfort him, only to bear witness, to hold a space for him, and to ease him back into the living.

"I was shot by Officer Babbit. Why did he shoot me? Was it because I lied to him? I saw light and it wasn't bad and I wasn't scared and I walked toward that light. Soon, there was nothing but light, and I was that light. I am dead. I don't feel dead. Things pass through me, but I don't feel dead. You, in your blindness and love, and you, in your ugliness and great care for my grandmother, brought me back, didn't you? What do I look like? What do I look like? What do I look like? Who am I now?" Victor trembled.

Grief was one thing, but fear was quite another, and not for a moment more did Elizabeth want her beloved Victor to be afraid. "Show him, Horace." And the monster gently helped Victor to his feet and then walked him slowly and steadily to a full-length mirror on the other side of the room. It was the longest walk of Victor's short life—or, rather, a longer walk than he had ever experienced in that other existence, in that other life. They arrived finally and stood together in front of their reflections.

"You are ugly," Victor said. "I am not. I look just like that other boy."

"You are that other boy, Victor."

"Pinky. Grandma. Thank you." His gratitude was a well—fathomless, inexhaustible, sweet.

"Now, my young friend, you must return home. This will be hard, but we want you to understand." Pinky's voice was grave, sober, and distinctly new.

Elizabeth spoke quietly, and Victor, while he knew she could not see, felt utterly seen. "Victor, you know your grandmother is dying. Pinky is going to help her do that. Do you understand?"

"You do not want to go mad. You do not want to live as only part of yourself."

"Yes. Yes."

"And will Pinky come back?"

"I can't do that, my little man. I can never go back."

"You want to be with Elizabeth."

"Yes. Yes."

"It's not at all about the fear of being punished."

"No. Remember the words of my father, your great-granddad: 'Soon,' he said, 'I shall die, and what I now feel be no longer felt. Soon these burning miseries will be extinct. I shall ascend my funeral pile triumphantly and exult in the agony of the torturing flames. The light of that conflagration will fade away; my ashes will be swept into the sea by the winds. My spirit will sleep in peace, or if it thinks, it will not surely think thus. Farewell.'"

"Great-Granddad was haunted by his actions, by grief, by anger. And if he had done what he set out to do, none of us would be here. All our lives would have burned in those flames. Your spirit is tired. You need to rest. I understand things," Victor said.

"Yes, you do."

"What is it, Pinky? What is it, Grandma? Show me how to do it. Teach me about reanimation. Tell me how to end suffering and stall death."

If silence is a river, that river flowed through the rooms of that cabin and into every nook and crevice, over every surface of counter or tabletop, under every bed, in between every piece of linen, across windowsill and lattice, and up against glass. Silence flowed against every thought and became a fourth guest, an invited one, a trusted one.

And this guest, silence, gave Victor the words. "Prolong life, and you prolong suffering and death. This is the end of the making of monsters," Victor said, "and both of you will become light together and forever. And yet." Here he stopped, looked directly into Pinky's eyes, and held his grandmother's hands together in his own. "I will be with you. I won't say good-bye. I love you both."

And there was a visitor, a friend of Pinky's from the neighboring village, a medicine man of eighty-three years, who arrived to take Victor away. Time passed, as it will do, but not much and too quickly, because within an hour, Pinky and Elizabeth were asleep side by side, nevermore to awake, the flames of their monster love mingling them together for eternity.

And within a few hours after the deaths of the monster and his bride, after an exhaustive but futile missing persons search of the immediate vicinity, and after a mother and father had resigned themselves to holding a corpseless funeral service for a child and two family members, Victor arrived on the doorstep alive, tearful but happy. "Mom and Dad," he said. "I'm home. Elizabeth and Pinky have become light." And there were embraces and tears and soon afterward a reunion with the girl that he loved. Victor and Shelley held on to each other, these two children, as if they would never let go, and Justine and Mark marveled at this, at one point almost believing that they were looking at one child, the two having finally and permanently joined forever into a single, loving entity.

A healthy, small-framed boy of about eleven years, confident, clean, eyes full of a still, much deeper water, stood up in front of Mrs. Flint's sixth grade class and said, as a matter of fact, but with a reverence palpable and precise, "Hello, my name is Victor, and I am named after the great Dr. Frankenstein. My great-granddaddy was his monster." What he did not say, was that he, himself, was a third-generation monster creation, that he had visited the land of the dead, that he didn't care for it much. and that he had decided, with the help of some friends, to return to the living. He was a monster not unlike other monsters, but he was certainly no devil—and he was, to be sure, the last of his kind on earth.